THE GIRL WHO CRIED MURDER

—

PAULA GRAVES

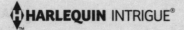

For Jenn and her mad brainstorming skills.

Recycling programs for this product may not exist in your area.

ISBN-13: 978-0-373-69942-1

The Girl Who Cried Murder

Copyright © 2016 by Paula Graves

This edition published by arrangement with Harlequin Books S.A.

For questions and comments about the quality of this book, please contact us at CustomerService@Harlequin.com.

Printed in U.S.A.

www.Harlequin.com

Paula Graves, an Alabama native, wrote her first book at the age of six. A voracious reader, Paula loves books that pair tantalizing mystery with compelling romance. When she's not reading or writing, she works as a creative director for a Birmingham advertising agency and spends time with her family and friends. Paula invites readers to visit her website, paulagraves.com.

Books by Paula Graves

Harlequin Intrigue

Campbell Cove Academy

Kentucky Confidential
The Girl Who Cried Murder

The Gates: Most Wanted

Smoky Mountain Setup
Blue Ridge Ricochet
Stranger in Cold Creek

The Gates

Dead Man's Curve
Crybaby Falls
Boneyard Ridge
Deception Lake
Killshadow Road
Two Souls Hollow

Bitterwood P.D.

Murder in the Smokies
The Smoky Mountain Mist
Smoky Ridge Curse
Blood on Copperhead Trail
The Secret of Cherokee Cove
The Legend of Smuggler's Cave

Visit the Author Profile page at Harlequin.com for more titles.

CAST OF CHARACTERS

Charlie Winters—Ten years ago, her best friend died in a hit-and-run accident. Charlie remembers little of the night, but she's convinced Alice's death was no accident. But will her decision to uncover the truth put her own life in danger?

Mike Strong—The Campbell Cove Academy instructor quickly realizes Charlie has an ulterior motive for taking his self-defense course. At first, he sees her as a puzzle to be solved, but when someone makes an attempt on her life, he makes her safety his number one priority.

Alice Bearden—She was keeping a secret from Charlie the night she died. What was it? Did it lead to her death?

Maddox Heller—One of Mike's bosses, Heller thinks Charlie's case is a good chance for Mike to hone his investigative skills.

Craig Bearden—Alice's father has made his daughter's death a driving reason for his run for political office. How will he react if it turns out her death wasn't what he thought?

Diana Bearden—Alice's mother has focused her life on her husband's political career. Is it a way to cope with the loss of her daughter? Or does she have her own secrets she wants to keep hidden?

Archer Trask—The police detective has never forgotten Alice's death. It was his first case as a detective, and he's never been convinced it was just an accident.

Randall Feeney—Craig Bearden's right-hand man will do anything to protect his boss. Does that include murder?

Chapter One

Mike Strong scanned the gymnasium for trouble, as he did every time he walked into a room. Fifteen years in the Marine Corps, in war zones from Africa to Central Asia, had taught him the wisdom of being alert and being prepared. All that training hadn't gone out the window when he'd left the Marines for life as a security consultant.

Especially at a company like Campbell Cove Security Services, where preparation for any threat was the company's mission statement.

The new 6:00 a.m. class was amateur hour—otherwise unschooled civilians coming in for an hour of self-defense and situational awareness training before heading off to their jobs at the factory or the grocery store or the local burger joint. In all likelihood, none of them would ever have to draw on their training in any meaningful way.

But all it took was once.

His later classes were more advanced, designed to give law enforcement officers and others with previous defense training new tactics to deal with the ever more complicated task of defending the US homeland. He'd come into this job thinking those classes would be more challenging.

But if the newest arrival was any indication, he might have been wrong about that.

She was tall, red-haired, pretty in a girl-next-door sort of way. Pert nose, a scattering of freckles in her pale complexion, big hazel-green eyes darting around the room with the same "looking for trouble" alertness he'd displayed a moment earlier. Beneath her loose-fitting T-shirt and snug-fitting yoga pants, she appeared lean and toned. A hint of coltish energy vibrated through her as she began a series of muscle stretches while her eyes continued their scan of the room.

What was she afraid of? And why did she expect to find it here?

Trying to ignore his sudden surge of adrenaline, he started with roll call, putting names to faces. There were only twelve students in the early-morning class, eight men and four women. The redhead, Charlie Winters, was the youngest of the group. The fittest, too.

Most of the others appeared to be fairly average citizens—slightly overweight, on the soft side both mentally and physically. Nice, good-hearted, but spoiled by living in a prosperous, free country where, until recent years, the idea of being the target of ruthless, fanatical predators had seemed as likely as winning the lottery.

"Welcome to Campbell Cove Academy's Basics

of Self-Defense class," he said aloud, quieting down the murmurs of conversation in the group. "Let's get started."

He followed Charlie Winters's earlier example and took the group through a series of stretching exercises. "I want you to get in the habit of doing these exercises every day when you get up," he told them. "Because you won't have time to do it when danger arises."

"How will stretching help us if some guy blows himself up in front of us?" one of the men grumbled as he winced his way through a set of triceps stretches. Mike searched his memory and came up with the name to go with the face. Clyde Morris.

"It won't, Clyde," he answered bluntly. "But it might help give you the strength and mobility to get the hell out of Dodge before your terrorist can trigger the detonator."

He didn't miss the quirk of Charlie Winters's eyebrows.

Did she disagree? Or did she have an agenda here that had nothing to do with preparing for terrorist threats?

Nothing wrong with that. There were plenty of reasons in a free society for a person to be ready for action.

But he found himself watching Charlie closely as they finished their stretches and he settled them on the mats scattered around the gymnasium floor. "Here's the thing you need to know about defending yourselves. Nothing I teach you here is a guarantee that you'll come out of a confrontation alive. So the first rule of self-defense is to avoid confrontations."

"That's heroic," Clyde Morris muttered.

"This class isn't about making heroes out of you. It's about keeping you alive so you can report trouble to people who have the training and weapons to deal with the situation. And then return home alive and well to the people who love you."

He let his gaze wander back to Charlie Winters's face as he spoke. Her gaze held his until the last sentence, when her brow furrowed and her lips took a slight downward quirk as she lowered her gaze to her lap, where her restless fingers twined and released, then twined again.

Hmm, he thought, but he didn't let his curiosity distract him further.

"I guess I should take a step backward here," he said. "Because there's actually something that comes before avoiding confrontation, and that's staying alert. Show of hands—how many of you have cell phones?"

Every person raised a hand.

"How many of you check your cell phone while walking down the street or entering a building? What about when you're riding in an elevator?"

All the hands went up again.

"That's what I'm talking about," he said. "How can you be alert to your surroundings if your face is buried in your phone?"

The hands crept down, the students exchanging sheepish looks.

"Look, we're fortunate to live in the time we do.

Technology can be a priceless tool in a crisis. Photographs and videos of incidents can be invaluable to investigators. Cell phones can bring help even when you're trapped and isolated. You can download apps that turn your phone into a flashlight. Your phone's signal can be used to find you when you're lost."

"Thank goodness. I was afraid you were going to tell us we had to lose our iPhones," one of the students joked.

"No, but I *am* suggesting you start thinking of it as a tool in your arsenal rather than a toy to distract and entertain you."

Again, he couldn't seem to stop his gaze from sliding toward Charlie's face. She met his gaze with solemn eyes, but her expression gave nothing else away. Still, he had a feeling that most of what he was telling the class were things she already knew.

So what was she doing here, taking this class?

Swallowing his frustration, he pushed to his feet and retrieved the rolling chalkboard he'd borrowed from one of the other instructors. "So, revised rule one—stay alert." He jotted the words on the board. "And now, let's talk about avoiding confrontations."

MIKE DISMISSED CLASS at seven. One or two students lingered, asking questions about some of the points he'd covered in class or what points he'd be covering in their class two days later. He answered succinctly, hiding his impatience. But it was with relief that the last student left and he hurried to his small office off the gymnasium. It was little more than a ten-by-ten box, but it had a desk, a phone and a window looking out on the parking lot.

He caught sight of Charlie Winters walking across the wet parking lot. She'd donned a well-worn leather jacket over her T-shirt and baggy sweatpants over her yoga pants, but there was no way to miss her dark red hair dancing in the cold wind blowing down the mountain or the coltish energy propelling her rapidly across the parking lot.

She stopped behind a small blue Toyota that had seen better days. But she didn't get into the car immediately. First, she walked all the way around the vehicle, examining the tires, peering through the windows, even dropping to the ground on her back and looking beneath the chassis.

Finally, she seemed to be satisfied by whatever she saw—or didn't see—and pushed back to her feet, dusting herself off before she got in the Toyota and started the engine.

As she drove away, Mike turned from the window, picked up the phone on the desk and punched in Maddox Heller's number. Heller answered on the second ring.

"It's Strong," Mike said. "You said to let you know if I had any concerns about the new class."

"And you do?"

He thought about it for a moment. "*Concern* may be too strong a word. At this point, I'd call it…curiosity."

"Close enough," Heller said. "So, you want a background check on someone?"

"Yes," Mike said after another moment of thought. "I do."

CHARLIE KEPT AN eye on the rearview mirror as she drove home as fast as she dared. She'd like to get a shower before her early-morning phone conference, and she was already going to be cutting it close. Could she really keep this up two days a week, given her boss's delight in scheduling early meetings?

Besides, after this morning's class, she wasn't even sure it was worth her time. All that stretching and they didn't do anything but go over the basic tenets of self-defense. On a chalkboard. Hell, she'd already covered those basics with a one-hour search of the internet. She didn't need an academic journey through the philosophy of protecting oneself.

She needed practical tools, damn it. Now. And she didn't want to spend the next few weeks twiddling her thumbs until Mr. Big Buff Badass deigned to detach himself from his chalkboard and teach them something they could actually use.

Channeling her frustration into her foot on the accelerator, she made it back to her little rental house on Sycamore Road with almost a half hour to spare. As had become habit, she waited at the front door for a few seconds, just listening.

There was a faint thump coming from inside, but she had two cats. Thumps didn't exactly come as a surprise.

Taking a deep breath, she tried the door. Still locked.

That was a good sign, wasn't it?

She unlocked the door and entered as quietly as she could, standing just inside the door and listening again.

There was a soft *prrrrup* sound as His Highness, her slightly cross-eyed Siamese rescue cat, slinked into the living room to greet her. He gave her a quizzical look before rubbing his body against her legs.

"Did you hold down the fort for me like I asked?" She bent to scratch his ears, still looking around for any sign of intrusion. But everything was exactly as she'd left it, as far as she could tell.

Maybe she was being paranoid. She couldn't actually prove that someone had been following her, could she?

There hadn't been a particular incident, just a slowly growing sense that she was being watched. But even that sensation had coincided with the first of the dreams, which meant maybe she was imagining it.

That could be possible, couldn't it?

She went from room to room, checking for any sign of an intruder. In her office, her other cat, Nellie, watched warily from her perch atop the bookshelf by her desk. If there had been an intruder, the nervous tortoiseshell cat would still be hidden under Charlie's bed. So, nobody had been in the house since she left that morning.

Beginning to relax, she took a quick shower and changed the litter box before she settled at her computer and joined the office conference call.

Because she worked for a government contractor, Ordnance Solutions, most of her conference calls consisted of a whole lot of officious blather and only a few nuggets of important information. This call was no different. But she wrote down those notes with admirable conscientiousness, if she did say so herself, especially with His Highness sitting on her desk and methodically knocking every loose piece of office equipment onto the floor.

She hammered out the project her bosses had given her during the conference call, a page-one revision of the latest operational protocols for disposal of obsolete ordnance from a recent spate of military base closures. Most of the changes had come after a close reading by the company's technical experts. Charlie was used to working her way through multiple revisions, especially if the experts couldn't come to an agreement on specific protocols.

Which happened several times a project.

Nellie, the cockeyed tortie, ventured into her office and hopped onto the chair next to her desk. She let Charlie give her a couple of ear scratches before contorting into a knot to start cleaning herself.

"Am I going crazy, Nellie?" Charlie asked.

Nellie angled one green eye at her before returning to her wash.

The problem was, Charlie didn't have a sounding board. Her family was a disaster—her father had died in a mining accident nearly twenty years ago, and her mother had moved to Arkansas with her latest husband a couple of years back. Two brothers in jail, two up in South Dakota trying to take advantage of the shale oil boom while it lasted, and her only sister had moved to California, where she was dancing at a club in Encino while waiting for her big break.

None of them were really bad people, not even the

two in jail. But none of them understood Charlie and her dreams. Never had, never would.

And they sure as hell wouldn't understand why she had suddenly decided to dig up decade-old bones.

And as for friends? Well, she'd turned self-imposed isolation into an art form.

She attached the revised ordnance disposal protocols to an email and sent it off to her supervisor, then checked her email for any other assignments that might have come through while she was working on the changes. The inbox was empty of anything besides unsolicited advertisements. She dumped those messages into the trash folder.

Then she opened her word processor program and took a deep breath.

It was now or never. If she was going to give up on the quest, this was the time. Before she made another trip to Campbell Cove Security Services and spent another dime on listening to Mr. Big Buff Badass lecture her on the importance of looking both ways before she crossed the street.

Pinching her lower lip between her teeth, she opened a new file, the cursor blinking on the blank page.

Settling her trembling hands on the keyboard, she began to type.

Two days before Christmas, nearly ten years ago, my friend Alice Bearden died. The police said it was an accident. Her parents believe the same. She had been drinking that night, cocktails aptly named

Trouble Makers. Strawberries and cucumbers muddled and shaken with vodka, a French aperitif called Bonal, lime juice and simple syrup. I looked up the recipe on the internet later.

I drank light beer. Just the one, as far as I remember. And that's the problem. For a long time, those three sips of beer were all I remembered about the night Alice died.

Then, a few weeks ago, the nightmares started.

I tried to ignore them. I tried to tell myself that they were just symptoms of the stress I've been under working this new job.

But that doesn't explain some of the images I see in my head when I close my eyes to sleep. It doesn't explain why I hear Alice whispering in my ear while the world is black around me.

"I'm sorry, Charlie," she whispers. "But I have to do the rest of this by myself."

What did she mean? What was she doing?

It was supposed to be a girls' night out, a chance to let down our hair before our last semester of high school sent us on a headlong hurdle toward college and responsibility. She was Ivy League bound. I'd earned a scholarship to James Mercer College, ten minutes from home.

I guess, in a way, it was also supposed to be the beginning of our big goodbye. We swore we'd keep in touch. But we all know how best intentions go.

I should have known Alice was up to something. She always was. She'd lived a charmed life—beautiful, sweet, the apple of her very wealthy daddy's eye.

She was heading for Harvard, had her life planned out. Harvard for undergrad, Yale Law, then an exciting career in the FBI.

She wanted to be a detective. And for a golden girl like Alice Bearden, the local police force would never do.

She had been full of anticipation that night. Almost jittery with it. We'd chosen a place where nobody knew who we were. We tried out the fake IDs Alice had procured from somewhere—"Don't ask, Charlie," she'd said with that infectious grin that could make me lose my head and follow her into all sorts of scrapes.

For a brief, exciting moment, I felt as if my life was finally going to start.

And then, nothing. No thoughts. Almost no memories. Just that whisper of Alice's voice in my ear, and the haunting sensation that there was something I knew about that night that I just couldn't remember.

I tried to talk to Mr. Bearden a few days ago. I called his office, left my name, told him it was about Alice.

He never called me back.

But the very next day, I had a strong sensation of being watched.

MIKE WRAPPED UP his third training session of the day, this time an internal refresher course for new recruits to the agency, around five that afternoon. He headed for the showers, washed off the day's sweat and changed into jeans and a long-sleeved polo. Civvies, he thought with a quirk of his lips that wasn't quite a smile. Because the thought of being a civilian again wasn't exactly a cause for rejoicing.

He'd planned on a career in the Marine Corps. Put in thirty or forty years or more, climbing the ranks, then retire while he was still young enough to enjoy it.

Things hadn't gone the way he planned.

There was a message light on his office phone. Maddox Heller's deep drawl on his voice mail. "Stop by my office on your way out. I may have something for you."

He crossed the breezeway between the gym and the main office building, shivering as the frigid wind bit at every exposed inch of his skin. He'd experienced much colder temperatures, but there was something about the damp mountain air that chilled a man to the bone.

Heller was on the phone when Mike stuck his head into the office. Heller waved him in, gesturing toward one of the two chairs that sat in front of his desk.

Mike sat, enjoying the comforting warmth of the place. And not just the heat pouring through the vents. There was a personal warmth in the space, despite its masculine simplicity. A scattering of photos that took up most of the empty surfaces in the office, from Heller's broad walnut desk to the low credenza against the wall. Family photos of Heller's pretty wife, Iris, and his two ridiculously cute kids, Daisy and Jacob.

Even leathernecks could be tamed, it seemed.

Maddox hung up the phone and shot Mike a look

of apology. "Sorry. Daisy won a spelling bee today and had to spell all the words for me."

Mike smiled. "How far the mighty warrior has fallen."

Heller just grinned as he picked up a folder lying in front of him. "One day it'll be you, and then you'll figure it out yourself."

"Figure out what?" he asked, taking the folder Heller handed him.

"That family just makes you stronger." Heller nodded at the folder. "Take a look at what our background check division came up with."

"That was quick." Mike opened the folder. Staring up at him was an eight-by-ten glossy photo of a dark-haired young woman. Teenager, he amended after a closer look. Sophisticated looking, but definitely young. She didn't look familiar. "This isn't the woman from my class."

"I know. Her name was Alice Bearden."

Mike looked up sharply. "Was?"

"She died about ten years ago. Two days before Christmas in a hit-and-run accident. The driver was never found."

Mike grimaced. So young. And so close to Christmas. "Bearden," he said. "Any relation to that Bearden guy whose face is plastered on every other billboard from here to Paducah?"

"Craig Bearden. Candidate for US Senate." Heller nodded toward the folder in Mike's lap. "Keep reading."

Mike flipped through the rest of the documents in

the file. They were mostly printouts of online news-paper articles about the accident and a few stories about Craig Bearden's run for the Senate. "Bearden turned his daughter's death into a political platform. Charming."

"His eighteen-year-old daughter obtained a fake ID so she could purchase alcohol in a bar. The bartender may have been fooled by the fake ID, but that doesn't excuse him from serving so much alcohol she was apparently too drunk to walk straight. And maybe her inebriation was what led her to wander into the street in front of a moving vehicle, but whoever hit her didn't stop to call for help."

"And he's now crusading against what exactly?"

"All of the above? The bartender was never charged, and the bar apparently still exists today, so I guess if he sued, he lost. Maybe this is his way of feeling he got some sort of justice for his daughter."

Mike looked at the photo of Alice Bearden again. A tragedy that her life was snuffed out, certainly. But he hadn't asked Heller to look into Alice Bearden's background.

"What does this have to do with Charlie Winters?" he asked.

"Read the final page."

Mike scanned the last page. It was earliest of the articles on the accident, he realized. The dateline was December 26, three days after the accident. He scanned the article, stopping short at the fourth paragraph.

Miss Bearden was last seen at the Headhunter Bar on Middleburg Road close to midnight, accompanied by another teenager, Charlotte Winters of Bagwell.

"Charlie Winters was with Alice when she died?"

"That seems to be the big question," Heller answered. "Nobody seems to know what happened between the time they left the bar and when Alice's body was found in the middle of the road a couple of hours later."

Mike's gaze narrowed. "Charlie refused to talk?"

"Worse," Heller answered. "I talked to the lead investigator interviewed in the article. He's still with the county sheriff's department and remembers the case well. According to him, Charlotte Winters claims to have no memory of leaving the bar at all. As far as she's concerned, almost the whole night is one big blank."

"And what does he think?"

"He thinks Charlie Winters might have gotten away with murder."

Chapter Two

Making four copies was overkill, wasn't it?

Charlie looked at the flash drive buried at the bottom of the gym bag's inner pocket. Were four copies a sign of paranoia?

"I wonder if Mike is married." The voice was female, conspiratorial and close by.

Charlie looked up to find one of her fellow students applying lipstick using a small compact mirror. Midthirties, decent shape, softly pretty. Kim, Charlie thought, matching the name from Monday's roll call to the face. She'd tried to memorize all the names and faces from the class. Partly as a game to relieve her boredom, but partly because the knowledge might come in handy someday.

Like during the zombie apocalypse?

Oh man. She *was* paranoid, wasn't she?

"I didn't expect him to be so hot," Kim said, punctuating the statement with the snap of her compact closing. "I didn't see a ring."

"Maybe he doesn't like to wear it when he's en-

gaging in self-defense activities." Charlie grimaced
at her lame response. Kim was clearly trying to be
friendly, seeking to engage Charlie with a topic they
might both find intriguing. And her response was to
cut her off at the knees?

"Maybe." Kim's smile faded. "Probably. A guy that
good-looking is either married by this age or gay."

"Or commitment-phobic," Charlie added.

"Honey, that can sometimes be a feature, not a
bug." Kim finger-combed her honey-blond hair and
smiled. "You ready?"

"Sure." Charlie walked with Kim out of the locker
room into the gymnasium, where about half the number of their Monday classmates were already waiting. Today, the gymnasium floor was covered nearly
wall-to-wall with padded floor mats. Apparently they
were going to do more than just take notes today.

Thank goodness.

Mike Strong stood against the front wall, flip-
ping through papers secured on a clipboard, his brow
furrowed with concentration. The light slanting in
from the east-facing windows bathed him in golden
warmth.

Beside Charlie, Kim released a gusty sigh. "Lord
have mercy."

Mike put the clipboard on the floor beside him
and looked up at the students gathering in front of
him. His gaze settled on Charlie for a moment, and
he smiled at her. To her surprise, her stomach turned
an unexpected flip.

"Oh, wow," Kim murmured. "Probably not gay, then."

"This is crazy," Charlie muttered, as much to herself as to Kim.

Mike checked his watch, the movement flexing his biceps and sending her stomach on another tumble. "It's time to get started. Everybody remember the stretches?"

Charlie's heart was beating far more quickly than her exertion level warranted. She forced herself to keep her gaze averted from Mike Strong's lean body and focused instead on maximizing the flex of her muscles.

But when she looked up again, Mike was walking slowly through the small clump of students, observing their efforts. He stopped in front of her and crouched, his voice lowering to a rumble. "You've done this before."

"High school gym," she answered, trying not to meet his gaze.

"Not college?"

Her gaze flicked up despite her intentions. "College, too. Core requirement."

His lips curved. "So I hear."

"You didn't have phys ed classes in college?"

"I went straight from high school to Parris Island," he said with a smile. "Lots and lots of phys ed, you could say."

She dropped her gaze again, but it was too late. Now she was picturing him in fatigues, out in the hot

South Carolina sun, sweat gleaming on his sculpted muscles and darkening the front of his olive drab T-shirt...

When she risked another peek, he'd moved on, walking from student to student, offering suggestions to improve their stretches. She let go of her breath, realizing her exhalation sounded suspiciously like the gusty sigh Kim had released earlier as they entered the gym.

"All right," Mike said a few minutes later, "I'm going to pair you up and we're going to talk about some of the basic escape moves. This really shouldn't be the first thing we do, but I can tell by the low attendance today that maybe you want a little less talk and a lot more action."

A few laughs greeted Mike's words, along with a few murmurs of agreement. Then everybody fell silent, watching with interest as Mike paired them up.

He left Charlie for last. There was nobody left to pair up with, she realized with a flutter of dismay. It was fifth-grade kickball all over again.

"You're with me," Mike said bluntly, nodding toward the front of the pack. She followed him with reluctance, revising her earlier thought. It wasn't kickball. It was Public Speaking 101, and it was Charlie's turn at the front of the class.

Heat flooded her cheeks, no doubt turning her pale skin bright red. Her hands trembled so hard she shoved them in the pockets of her sweatpants and tried not to meet the gaze of anyone else in the gym.

"If you've read any books or watched any movies

or TV shows, you've probably heard of the vulnerable spots on an assailant and some of the ways to target them. Knee to the groin. Foot to the instep or the knee. Fingers to the eyes or heel of the hand to the cartilage of the nose." There were soft groans at the images those words invoked. "Those are all vulnerable targets on an attacker, true. But how easy is it for a small person to do damage to a larger person, even targeting those areas? That's what we're going to experiment with today."

Charlie realized he'd paired people up by size, small with large. At the moment, most of the larger people in the pairings were looking around with alarm.

Mike nodded toward the side of the room, where a man stood in the doorway next to what looked like a large laundry bin. "This is Eric Brannon. He's a doctor. I thought y'all might want him to stick around for this."

Eric grinned. Charlie's classmates didn't.

"He's also got some equipment to hand out."

Eric reached into the bin and pulled out something that looked like a cross between a life jacket and a catcher's chest guard. He handed it to the man standing closest to him and continued through the other students, passing out padding to the larger of each pair.

Eric stopped before giving anything to Mike. Charlie looked up at the instructor, one eyebrow arched.

Mike grinned back at her, then turned to the class. "We're going to start with the first thing you need to know how to deal with—someone grabbing you."

Without warning, he reached out and wrapped his arm around Charlie's shoulders, pulling her back hard against his chest.

She gasped, caught entirely flat-footed, and began struggling on instinct. His grip tightened and he lifted her off her feet.

Her vision seemed to darken around the edges, sight becoming a single pinpoint of light as anger fought with panic.

Damn it, Charlie. Do something!

She was back in a darkened alley outside the Head-hunter Bar. The world was tilted and spinning, like she was stuck on a merry-go-round twirling at an impossible rate of speed. She couldn't breathe. Couldn't think.

She kicked her heel backward, hitting his shin with a glancing blow that didn't even elicit a grunt. His grip tightened. Clawing at his rock-hard arms with her fingers had no effect at all. She stamped her heel down on his foot, but his boots were hard and her foot glanced off, which was probably the only thing that saved her from a broken foot of her own.

I'm sorry, Charlie, but I have to do the rest of this by myself. Alice's whispered words rang in her ears, clarity in a world of insanity.

She stopped struggling, and the grip on her shoulders loosened. The world seeped back in brilliant light and color, and panic won over anger. She dropped her whole weight downward, slipping from his grip, and rolled as hard as she could into his knee. The move sent Mike sprawling to the mat, and Charlie scrambled to her feet and ran for the door, her whole body rattling with the need to escape at all costs.

Eric Brannon caught her arm, pulling her to a jerky halt. She was about to fight when she realized he was smiling at her.

She made herself stop running. It was just a class. Just a game, really.

No dark alley. No woozy world. No whispers in her ear.

"Nice job," Eric murmured, his blue eyes bright with amusement.

She looked at Mike, who was back on his feet. Unlike Eric, he wasn't smiling. Instead, he was watching her with a knowing wariness that made her stomach twist. After a moment, however, his expression cleared and he motioned her over. "That was actually a pretty good example of one of the things we're going to talk about today," he said as she walked with reluctance to his side. "What Charlie did was to use deception to change her circumstances. The more she struggled, the tighter I held her. When she seemed to give up, to stop struggling, I loosened my grip. It's a natural response—assailants can tire of the struggle as well, even if they're considerably stronger and larger than their targets."

Charlie slanted him a skeptical look. He didn't look as if he'd tired at all. She was pretty sure he could have held her in check a whole lot longer than he had.

He met her gaze, his smile seemingly warm. But he was smiling only with his mouth. His green eyes were narrowed and still wary.

"The other thing she did is what I'd like to address today," he added. "As soon as she was in the position to do so, Charlie bowled me over. She used her full weight to catch me off balance and send me to the ground. And yet I outweigh her by at least eighty pounds. Probably more. Which goes to show, even if your assailant is larger than you, you have more leverage than you think."

Charlie wrapped her arms around her, feeling exposed and vulnerable. She edged back toward the wall as Mike Strong walked the rest of the students through an attacker's vulnerable points and how to strike back at those areas more effectively.

"Put your weight into everything you do. If you can hurt them, you're that much closer to knocking them down and getting away. Now, I want the bigger partners to suit up and play the part of the attacker. Smaller partners, go after the pressure points. For now, avoid the nose and face. What I want you to practice is putting your full weight into everything you do. Turn your body into a weapon."

The rest of the group got started. There was a lot of noise, most of it self-conscious laughter. Charlie watched the others for a moment, until she felt Mike's gaze on her.

She looked at him. He was studying her as if she were some scientific experiment on display. Her cheeks, which had finally started to cool off, went hot again.

She half expected him to ask her what the hell had

happened when he grabbed her. Surely he'd seen that her panic had been real.

But when he spoke, he asked, "Have you had any self-defense training before?"

"I was a skinny freckled redhead in public school," she answered, going for levity. "I had twelve years of self-defense training."

He smiled faintly. "Formal training?"

"I've read a lot. Watched a lot of videos on the 'net."

"So you've done the mental work. Just not the physical."

"Something like that."

"I have an intermediate class that meets Tuesday and Thursday afternoons at four. Do you think you could make that class?"

He thought she should go into an intermediate class? Why? She hadn't exactly covered herself in glory so far.

"I have a flexible work schedule," she said finally, wondering just what an intermediate self-defense class would entail. "But I'm really just a beginner," she added quickly. "I just got lucky earlier."

"That wasn't luck. That was your instincts kicking in. You've internalized the lessons in your head. Now your body needs to learn how to do the things your brain has already processed. But there's no need for you to start from the beginning when you'd be learning a lot more in an advanced class."

Charlie narrowed her eyes, not sure she trusted Mike Strong's motives for wanting to move her out of the beginner class. She'd seen the wariness in his eyes earlier. And even now, there was a hint of tension in his jaw when he spoke, as if he was trying to hide his real thoughts.

"You think I could keep up?" she asked.

"I think so. If you feel differently after a class or two, you can always come back to this class."

"And is self-defense the only thing you learn in the intermediate class?" she asked before she thought the question through.

His brow creased. "What else would you be looking to learn?"

She cleared her throat. "I just meant—there's more to protecting yourself than just being able to get out of physical situations, isn't there?"

Mike looked at her for a long moment, then jerked his attention away, his gaze shifting across the gymnasium, as if he'd just remembered that he was supposed to be supervising the class. "Darryl, the padding doesn't mean you can be a brute. This is our first time out. Try not to break Melanie's neck, how about it?"

Charlie watched the rest of the class giggle and grunt their way through the exercises while Mike went through the group, offering suggestions and gentle correction. Right about now, she'd give anything to be one of them, one of the group instead of standing here like a flagpole in the middle of the desert, visible from every direction.

Mike finally wandered back to where she stood. "The intermediate class is mainly about physical self-defense," he finally answered in response to her earlier question. "But if you have any specific questions about how to protect yourself, you can always ask."

"If I do, I will," she said, not sure she meant it. He was giving off all the vibes of a man who was suspicious of her motives, and considering her little freak-out a few minutes ago, she couldn't really blame him.

The last thing she needed to do was pique his curiosity.

"So, I'll see you tomorrow afternoon in the intermediate course?" Mike glanced at her, his expression suggesting he wasn't sure she'd say yes.

But he wanted her to say yes, she realized.

The question was, why?

"Yes," she said finally. "I'll be there."

"Can you stick around for the rest of the class?"

The twinkle in his eyes gave her pause, but she made herself smile. "Should I say no?"

He laughed. "There are still a few moves I need to show the class. And since you're here…"

"I get to be the damsel in distress?"

He shook his head slowly. "The one thing I'm pretty sure you've never been, Charlie, is the damsel in distress."

"So, WHAT DO you think?"

Mike turned his head away from the window, dragging his gaze from Charlie's little blue Toyota. She hadn't emerged from the gymnasium yet; when he'd left, she'd been talking to a couple of the other students.

He met Maddox Heller's gaze. "I don't know. She's hard to read."

"In what way?"

He thought about her reaction to being called to the front of the class that morning. "She can be shy. And then turn around and be assertive. But there was something that happened today—I'm not sure how to describe it."

"Give it a shot."

"I was demonstrating how quickly an assailant could strike. Partly as an example, but also because I wanted to know how she'd react. I expected her to fight."

"And she didn't?"

"No, she fought. But there was something about the way she did it. It was as if she was somewhere else. Seeing something else."

Heller's expression was thoughtful. "Post-traumatic stress?"

"Maybe. She was able to keep herself together enough to escape my grasp, though. And she did it pretty well. Bowled me over."

"There wasn't a lot in the background check other than what I told you. The sheriff's department never liked her story that she could remember nothing. But I don't know if that's because of who she is. Or, more to the point, who her family is."

"Who are they?"

"The Winters, according to my source with the local law, are one of those families that just spell trouble. Two of her brothers are in jail. Daddy died in a mining accident when they were young, and apparently Mama tried and failed to replace him with a series of men who all brought their own brand of trouble to the family."

"Does Charlie have a record?"

"Nothing as an adult. If she had any record as a juvenile, it's sealed."

"I've moved her up to my intermediate class," Mike said. "The beginner class will just bore her. She might quit."

"And you don't want that?"

He didn't. "Something strange is going on with that woman. I don't know what yet. But I think it's in our interests to find out what it is."

He turned back to the window. Charlie was out there now, unlocking the driver's door of the Toyota. She slid behind the steering wheel and pulled out of the parking lot, heading onto Poplar Road.

Mike's gaze started to follow the car up the road, but something in the parking space she'd just vacated snagged his attention. There was a wet spot on the pavement beneath where the Toyota had been parked.

Right about the place where her brake line should be.

He muttered a curse and strode past Heller, already running as he hit the exit. He skidded to a stop at the empty parking place and crouched to look at the fluid on the ground.

Definitely brake fluid.

He gazed at the road, spotting the Corolla just as it started the climb up the mountain.

Without a pause for thought, he pulled his keys from his pocket and sprinted toward his truck.

THE TOYOTA HAD to be on its last legs. Fifteen years old, well-used before she'd ever bought it, the little blue Corolla had put up with a lot in the five years since she'd bought it with cash from a small used car lot over in Mercerville. The heating and air were starting to falter—never good in the dead of winter or the dog days of summer. And as she crested the mountain and started down the other side, she realized her brakes felt unresponsive, spongy beneath her foot.

That was not good.

She dropped the Corolla to a lower gear, and the vehicle's speed slowed, but only a little. She thought about putting it in Neutral, but in the back of her mind, she had a fuzzy memory that doing so wasn't the answer.

Damn. Why hadn't she read that road safety brochure her insurance company had sent out last month?

Fortunately, there wasn't much in the way of traffic on the two-lane road, but she was fast approaching a four-way stop at the bottom of the hill. There were a handful of cars clustered at the intersection, far enough away now that they looked more like specks than vehicles.

But that was changing quickly.

She dropped to an even lower gear and gave her brakes a few quick, desperate pumps. They were entirely unresponsive now.

Don't panic don't panic don't panic...

The roar of an engine approaching behind her took her eyes off the road to check the rearview mirror. There was a large pickup truck coming up fast behind her. Suddenly, it swung left, around her, and whipped into the lane in front of her.

What the hell was that idiot doing?

The truck slowed as it moved in front of her, and on instinct, she stamped on her useless brakes. The front of her car bumped hard into the back bumper of the truck, bounced and hit a second time. A third time, then a fourth, each bounce less jarring until her front bumper settled against the back of the truck.

The pickup slowed to a stop, bringing her Corolla to a stop, as well. She turned on her hazard lights and put her car in Park, setting the parking brake to make sure it didn't move any farther downhill.

The driver's door of the pickup opened, and a tall, lean-muscled figure got out and turned to face her with a grim smile.

Mike Strong.

What the hell was going on?

Chapter Three

"The brake line's been cut." Bill Hardy, the mechanic at Mercerville Motors, who'd taken a look at the Corolla's brake system, showed Charlie the laceration in the line.

Charlie stared at it in horrified fascination, trying not to relive those scary moments as she'd struggled to bring her car under control on the downhill stretch of Poplar Road. If Mike Strong hadn't pulled his driving trick to bring her car to a stop—

Don't think about it.

"How could that have happened?" she asked Bill.

"Well, maybe you could have kicked up a sharp rock or a piece of metal in the road," Bill said doubtfully.

"But you don't think so?"

"Honestly, if I didn't know better, I'd think this was a deliberate cut." He gave her a sidelong look. "You haven't made any enemies lately, have you, Charlie?"

Had she?

She glanced toward the tiny waiting area, where

Mike Strong sat in one of the steel-and-plastic chairs pushed up against the wall across from the vending machine. She'd told him he needn't wait for her, but he'd insisted. And given that he'd more or less saved her life this morning, she could hardly quibble.

"No, no new enemies," she said.

Except, she supposed, whoever had killed Alice.

She turned her head to look at Mike again and found him standing in the open doorway between the waiting area and the garage. "Any news?"

"Brake line's cut," Bill said shortly before Charlie could stop him.

Mike's eyebrows came together over his nose. "On purpose?"

"Hard to say with certainty, but it's possible." Bill looked at Charlie. "What do you want me to do? You've got a little body work needs doing on the front now, and the brake line needs replacing—"

"Can I have the damaged brake line?" Mike asked.

Charlie frowned at him. "Why?"

Mike's green eyes met hers. "Evidence."

Bill's brown eyes darted from Charlie's face to Mike's and back again. "Should I call the cops?"

"No," Charlie and Mike said in unison.

"Okay, then." Bill licked his lips, looking confused.

"Fix the body damage and replace the brake line," Charlie said. "And preserve the brake line in case we need to let someone examine it to establish whether or not the cut was intentional."

"Will do," Bill said with a nod. "Listen, it's probably

going to take me a few days to get this done. You gonna have a way to get around?"

"I'll figure out something." Charlie nibbled her lip, wondering if she could make do with her bike for a few days. She didn't have any meetings scheduled at work for the next couple of weeks, so she didn't have to worry about a commute. There was a small grocery store a half mile from her house, so she and the cats wouldn't starve. Even Campbell Cove Academy was within a mile's ride. It would be good exercise.

"I can give you a ride home, at least," Mike said.

"Thanks."

"What *are* you going to do for wheels?" Mike asked as they walked to his truck.

"I have a bike."

He slanted a look at her as he unlocked the passenger door of the truck. "What if it rains?"

There was no what-if; rain fell practically every week in the mountains, and often multiple days a week. She hadn't really thought about rain, but that was what raincoats were for, right? "I'll deal."

He waited for her to fasten her seat belt before he started the engine. The dashboard clock read 11:35 and, to her chagrin, her stomach gave a little growl in response. Breakfast had been a long time ago.

"I could go for an early lunch," he murmured, sounding amused. "You wanna come?"

She looked at him through the corner of her eye, trying to assess his motives. "To lunch? With you?"

His sunglasses had mirror lenses, so she couldn't be sure his smile made it all the way to his eyes. "I suppose we could sit apart, if you like. Though that seems like a waste of a table."

Mayfair Diner was little more than a hole-in-the-wall, one of three storefronts that filled the one-story brick building on the corner of Mayfair Lane and Sycamore Road. Charlie ate there often, since her house was just a short drive down Sycamore. By now, everybody who worked there knew her by name and called out greetings when they entered.

"What's good here?" Mike asked as they headed for the counter.

"Depends on how much weight you want to gain."

He smiled at her blunt answer and looked up at the big menu board. "How are the omelets?"

"I like them," she answered with a little shrug. "The cheese-and-bacon ones are particularly good."

"I bet."

The counter waitress, a plump, pretty woman in her forties named Jean, smiled as she approached to take their order. "Hey, Charlie, what can I get for you and your friend today?"

"I'll have a grilled cheese with chips and a pickle, and iced coffee with cream and sugar," Charlie said.

"And you, hon?" Jean looked at Mike, her voice instantly flirtatious.

"I'll have a veggie omelet and a small fresh fruit cup," he ordered. "And water to drink."

Disgustingly healthy, Charlie thought. Would explain his smokin'-hot body, though.

"Find yourself a seat, and I'll send someone out with your orders in a few minutes," Jean said with one last flirtatious smile at Mike before she turned to clip their orders to the chef's order wheel.

Charlie and Mike settled in a corner booth. He took the bench seat that faced the door, she noticed. Always on the lookout for trouble?

An uncomfortable silence lingered between them for a moment before Mike broke it in a gravelly murmur. "You didn't seem that surprised when the guy at the garage thought your brake line had been cut."

She looked up sharply. "What's that supposed to mean?"

He shrugged. "If someone told me my brake line had been cut…"

"You'd start with your self-defense class roster?" She flashed him a cheeky grin to hide her own sense of unease with his question.

He grinned back. "Probably."

What she didn't want to admit, even to herself, was that there might be someone out there who wanted her dead. For most of her life she'd been fairly invisible, by design. Her ne'er-do-well brothers had brought more than their share of ignominy to the family name. Better not to draw any attention at all than the kind her brothers had managed to elicit.

A smiling teenage girl came over with their orders on a large tray, saving Charlie from having to find something else to say to break the silence. The girl eyed Mike with starstruck shyness, giggling a little as he smiled his thanks. Charlie wasn't sure the girl even realized there was a second person at the table.

"Does that happen often?" she asked, taking a sip of her iced coffee.

Mike looked up from his plate. "Does what happen?"

Charlie nodded toward the waitress who was still darting quick looks toward their table as she talked with another server. "Googly-eyed females growing tongue-tied in your presence."

He frowned. "Never noticed."

Of course he hadn't. She changed the subject back to the topic of the hour. "How on earth did you even notice that brake fluid in the parking lot?"

"I happened to be looking out the window when you drove away. There was a big puddle of fluid underneath the car, so I thought I should check it out. When I realized it was brake fluid—"

"You hopped in your truck and raced to my rescue?"

"Seemed like the thing to do."

"When you first whipped around in front of me, I thought you were a maniac." She shook her head. "That was kind of a crazy thing to do."

"Blame the academy. Crisis driving is one of the things we're trained to do, you know."

"Does the Campbell Cove Academy teach those skills to civilians, too?"

"Only to professional security personnel at the moment," he said with a shake of his head. "It's an intense and expensive course, and most civilians won't have any need to learn the skills."

"Not sure I agree with that," she said wryly.

He leaned a little closer, lowering his voice. "You

really have no idea who might have tampered with your car?"

"Why would I?"

"You just started taking a self-defense course, and now your vehicle is sabotaged. I have to wonder if there's a correlation."

She pretended not to understand. "You think someone messed with my car because I'm taking a self-defense course?"

He frowned. "Don't be obtuse. I'm asking if the reason you're taking a self-defense course has anything to do with why someone might tamper with your brakes. Have you been threatened? A stalker or a disgruntled ex?"

"Nobody's threatened me."

He sat back, studying her through narrowed eyes. "I'm not sure you can say that with a straight face after today. Assuming your mechanic is right about how the brake line was cut."

"I don't know who would want to hurt me," she said firmly.

That was the problem, wasn't it? She didn't know who would want to hurt her any more than she knew who would have hurt Alice. But someone had. She was more convinced of that fact than ever.

"Okay," Mike said after a long silence. "But I think you should be careful anyway. Maybe this morning was a warning shot."

"I'm planning to be careful."

"You still planning on trying to get around by bike?"

"Or on foot. I work from home, and most of the places I go on any given day I can reach by walking."

"Not sure that's a good idea."

"It's not like my track record in a car is exactly stellar after this morning," she joked.

He didn't smile. "Are you going to be at my class tomorrow afternoon?"

She shook her head. "The academy is a little too far away for a bike ride. Maybe I can pick up the class the next time you offer it."

"You'll have your car back soon. I can give you a ride to the class until then. Just be ready about a half hour early and I'll swing by to pick you up."

She narrowed her eyes. "Why? Why would you do that?"

"Because I think you need it. It's not like it's a big problem for me to give you a ride."

She nibbled her lower lip, considering his offer. He was right about one thing—she'd like to know how to protect herself in a pinch. Wasn't that why she'd picked up the self-defense class in the first place?

But Mike Strong was taking a peculiar amount of personal interest in her well-being, and she had a feeling it wasn't a matter of altruism. He had seemed suspicious of her the very first class, hadn't he?

A new thought occurred to her. Could Mike have been the person who'd tampered with her brakes?

"What is it?" he asked, looking suddenly concerned.

She schooled her own features, trying to hide her doubts. "Nothing. I was just remembering this morning. Can't seem to shake it."

"That's natural," he assured her with an easy smile. "That had to be a pretty terrifying few minutes."

"Definitely." She forced a smile. "And you're right. I should be back in my car in a week, so there's no real reason not to try to keep up with the self-defense courses."

His concerned expression had cleared completely, now that he'd gotten his way. "So I'll pick you up about thirty minutes before class starts? I like to get there early and do some prep work, if that's okay."

"That's fine," she assured him, smiling again. "Do I need to bring anything besides me and my sparkling personality?"

He grinned. "That should be all you need. We'll supply the rest."

At her insistence, Mike let her pay for lunch. But he insisted on coming into her house with her instead of just dropping her off.

"You didn't think someone was going to cut your brake line, either," he argued when she told him he was being paranoid. "I'd like to be sure you're not about to walk in on an intruder alone."

Grimacing, Charlie gave in, hoping she hadn't left the place in too much of a mess that morning. Fortunately, neither of her cats had pulled one of their insane stunts, such as trailing toilet paper around the house or dumping over all the potted plants.

The house was silent and still when they entered. No sign of intruders. And thanks to Mike's presence, no sign of the cats, either, save for His Highness's well-worn catnip mouse sitting in the middle of the living room floor.

"You have a pet?" Mike asked, picking up the toy.

"Two. Cats. Currently in hiding, since you're here."

He gave a nod of understanding.

A quick walk-through seemed to satisfy his need to play protector, and Charlie walked him to the door. "Thanks for your help this morning."

"I'm glad I was able to help." He looked up and down the street behind him, as if he expected trouble. But the street was as quiet and normal as the house. "See you tomorrow afternoon?"

"Yes. Thanks."

"Lock the door behind me." He started down the porch steps and crossed to his truck, turning as he reached the vehicle. "Lock the door, Charlie," he repeated, nodding toward her.

She closed the door and engaged the lock as he asked.

But as the sound of the truck's engine faded to silence, she realized she didn't feel any safer.

MIKE PULLED OFF the road onto the gravel-paved scenic overlook and got out of the truck, pacing with restless energy to the steel railing that kept visitors from stepping off the edge of the bluff. He curled his fists around the top rail, ignoring the burn of the cold steel against his bare palms. If anything, the discomfort helped him focus his scattered thoughts.

Lunch with Charlie Winters hadn't gone the way he'd expected. He'd figured her obvious shakiness after the near disaster with her car might have made her drop her guard. He could use her rattled state to coax a few secrets out of her, and then he'd have a better idea what her real agenda might be.

Instead, not only had she managed to keep all her secrets, he was now convinced she was hiding even more than he'd suspected.

And instead of probing her story, trying to break through her wall of protection, he'd just sat back and listened. Because he liked to hear her talk. He liked the soft twang of her Kentucky accent, the way her lips quirked when she shot him a quizzical smile. He liked the twinkle in her eyes when he said something she found amusing. He liked the way she smelled—clean and crisp, like a garden kissed by the morning sun.

And the fact that he could come up with a description as ridiculous as "a garden kissed by the morning sun" was why he felt as if he'd just walked into a booby trap and all that was left for him to do was curl up in a ball and wait for the explosion.

He took several deep breaths and gazed across the hazy blue mountains that stretched out for miles before the first sign of a town showed up in the distance. Maybe he was just making too much of the way Charlie was making him feel. It had been a while since he'd really let himself think about a woman as anything other than a fellow soldier or one of the faceless, nameless civilians his orders had required him to protect from the enemy.

After his career as a Marine had ended and he'd

entered the civilian force, it had taken a while just to get back into the swing of a life that didn't include gunfire, explosions and endless miles of dirt and sand. He hadn't wanted to look within the walls of the academy for a woman to share his bed and he'd been so focused on his job that he hadn't really looked outside the academy walls, either.

What he needed was a real date. A woman, a nice dinner, maybe some dancing or a movie. Ease into a love life again. No strings, no pressure. No bright hazel eyes making his stomach feel as if it were turning inside out.

Maybe Heller's wife had a friend he could meet. Weren't women always trying to fix up their husbands' single friends?

He pulled out his phone to record a reminder to feel Iris Heller out about her single friends the next time he ran into her, but he saw there was a "missed call" message. It was from someone named Randall Feeney.

For a moment, he thought it must have been a wrong number. Then he remembered the phone call he'd made before he'd set out on his search for Charlie Winters. He took a chance and called Feeney back.

"Randall Feeney," a man answered. In the background, Mike heard the low hum of voices and the ringing of phones—the sounds of a busy office.

"Mr. Feeney, this is Mike Strong from Campbell Cove Security Services. You just called my cell phone."

"Right, because you called the campaign office wanting to talk to someone about Alice Bearden." The man's voice lowered a notch. "May I ask the reason for your interest?"

Mike had already prepared his answer, but he'd really hoped to talk to Craig Bearden himself. "I'd rather discuss it with Mr. Bearden."

"That's not going to happen," Feeney said firmly. "However, I'm Mr. Bearden's executive aide and a longtime friend of the family. If you have any questions about Alice or the tragedy of her death, I may be able to help you. But I'd prefer to meet in person. Can you be at the campaign headquarters in Mercerville tomorrow afternoon? Say, around three?"

"I'm sorry, I'll be busy then. What about later today? Maybe around six?"

There was a brief pause before Feeney agreed. "Six is doable. I'll meet you here at the campaign headquarters. Do you know where that is?"

"I do." He'd looked up the address before he'd made the first call.

"I have to admit, however, I'm a little puzzled why someone from your company would have any interest in what happened to Alice," Feeney added, sounding wary.

"It may have some bearing on a case we're helping to investigate," Mike said, keeping his tone noncommittal. "I'll know more when we speak."

"Very well, then. See you at six." Feeney hung up without any further goodbye.

Mike pocketed his phone, feeling a little less rattled than before, now that he had a mission. He'd go talk to Randall Feeney, hear the story of Alice

Bearden's death from someone who, as Feeney had proclaimed, was close to the family. If anyone would know what role Charlie Winters might have had in the death of Alice, it would be Craig Bearden's personal assistant.

Maybe Feeney could shed some much-needed light on what Charlie Winters really wanted from her self-defense classes at Campbell Cove Academy.

Then Mike could put the confounding woman out of his head for good.

Chapter Four

If there was one thing Charlie was good at, it was making lists. Grocery lists, to-do lists, Christmas lists—she found satisfaction in writing down things that needed to be addressed and marking them off when she'd tackled and conquered them.

Today's list was a to-do list of sorts, though marking off the items would take more than just a few hours of concentration and dedication.

First item on the list was already underway, at least. Learn the basics of self-defense. Couldn't really mark it off yet, since she was only two classes into her lessons. But maybe if she agreed to Mike Strong's offer to join his intermediate class, she'd reach that particular goal more quickly.

On the other hand, what if he turned out to be a problem? He was already giving her strange looks, as if he knew her reason for taking a self-defense class wasn't as simple as the fact that she lived alone and wanted to be able to protect herself.

Was there something else on the list she could

start to tackle before she was finished with her self-defense classes?

The second item was a possibility: make another attempt to talk to Mr. Bearden. Alice's father.

She knew there wasn't any chance of talking to Alice's mother, Diana. The woman hadn't been able to look at Charlie at the funeral, even though she'd always been kind to Charlie before Alice's death.

To be honest, Charlie hadn't been that eager to face Diana Bearden, either. Fair or not, Charlie had always felt a great deal of guilt for what had happened to Alice, too.

But maybe she could handle Craig Bearden. Assuming she could get the man to talk to her after all this time. It had been years since she'd seen Craig Bearden, if you didn't count the signs and billboards that had cropped up all over eastern Kentucky since he'd announced his run for the US Senate. And even if they'd been closer, how easy would it be to get any face time with a political candidate?

Besides, they hadn't exactly parted company as friends. He'd never said the words aloud, but Charlie believed he'd blamed her for Alice's accident. Most people had. After all, Charlie was one of the Winters from Bagwell. The wrongest of the wrong sides of the tracks.

And her childhood talent for elaborate story fabrication hadn't exactly helped her case, had it? *That Charlotte Winters never met a truth she couldn't gussy up.*

Mr. Bearden hadn't wanted to listen when she'd

told him she thought Alice had met up with someone else that night at the bar. Facing the tragic death of his eighteen-year-old daughter had been horrific enough.

He'd never been willing to contemplate the idea that what happened to his little girl might not have been an accident.

Charlotte hadn't wanted to believe it, either. It was one bald truth she'd had no desire to doctor up and make more interesting.

But after a while, the nightmares had started. It had taken a while to realize the fragmented scenes of fear and confusion were actually memories that had been buried somewhere in her subconscious.

That night at the Headhunter Bar, three sips of light beer were all Charlie could remember for years. After that, nothing. No memories. No sensations or sounds or smells. Nothing but a terrifying blank.

Until the dreams had started.

She didn't imagine she could have gotten drunk that night, because she had never been much of a drinker. Thanks to her two jailbird brothers, she'd taken her first taste of alcohol at the age of twelve. The hard stuff, hard enough to turn her off alcohol for years. When she hit high school, she'd occasionally drunk a beer when she was with other people— peer pressure, she guessed—but she had no taste for it, and she certainly wouldn't have drunk enough to get so wasted that she'd black out.

But the alternative had been far more horrifying to contemplate, so she hadn't. She'd gone along with the accepted story—two teenage girls buy fake

IDs and go drinking. One passed out and the other wandered drunkenly into the path of a car and died of her injuries. Alice's blood alcohol level had been elevated—.09, which was over the legal limit to be considered impaired.

But had she been impaired enough to walk in front of a car without trying to escape?

The police had used a breathalyzer on Charlie when they'd shown up to ask questions about Alice's death, but several hours had already passed since she'd awakened, half-frozen and disoriented, in her backyard.

Charlie rubbed her forehead, feeling the first grind of a tension headache building behind her eyes. She drew a line through goal number two—speaking to Craig Bearden—and rewrote the goal several steps down the page. It was way too early to talk to Alice's father about her death, especially now that he had made increasing penalties for both serving alcohol to minors and reckless driving laws a significant part of his political platform.

Besides, she'd called him not that long ago, without getting any response. Well, unless you counted brake tampering. And did she really think Craig Bearden would do something like that?

Nellie looked up with alarm when Charlie scraped her chair back quickly, bumping up against the bookcase where she perched. His Highness merely blinked at her, uninterested, from his sunny spot on the windowsill.

"Mama needs to get out of here," Charlie told

them, going as far as to grab her jacket before she realized she couldn't leave. Beyond the work she still had to complete before quitting time this afternoon, she no longer had a car at her disposal. And the bike wasn't exactly a safe alternative, was it?

An image flashed through her head. Alice lying dead on the road, her body battered and broken from the collision with a car. Blood seeping from her head, thick, dark and shiny on the pavement.

She sat down abruptly, her limbs suddenly shaky. Why was that image of Alice's broken body in her mind in the first place? She hadn't been there when Alice died.

Had she?

MIKE REACHED THE Craig Bearden for Senate headquarters in Mercerville with only a few minutes to spare, but he used every one of those extra minutes trying to get his mind off those terrifying moments when he'd thought he wasn't going to catch up to Charlie Winters before her runaway car slammed into the line of vehicles waiting at the four-way stop.

It had been close. Too close. And strangely, the time that had passed between their close call and now only seemed to intensify his memories of those heart-racing seconds.

Catching up, then passing her to get in front. Trying to time his slowdown—not too sudden, or the impact of her car against his might have injured her. But if he hadn't slowed down soon enough, they might have run out of pavement between them and the cars on the road ahead.

It had been a nerve-racking few minutes, and he was in no hurry to repeat the experience anytime soon.

The clock on his dashboard clicked over to 5:59. He made the effort to shake off the unsettling memories. Put on his game face.

It was showtime.

Bearden's campaign office was a storefront with wide plate glass windows and a glass door, all imprinted with Bearden for Senate in big red letters. The place was still bustling with staff and volunteers, including an energetic young woman in jeans wearing a large round Bearden for Senate button on her sweater. "Bearden for Senate. Would you like to sign up to volunteer?"

"Actually, I'm here to see Randall Feeney. Is he here?"

The girl looked sheepish. "Oh no, I'm sorry. You're Mr. Strong, aren't you? Mr. Feeney was called away unexpectedly and I was supposed to call you to ask if he could reschedule for another day, but it just got so busy."

Mike suppressed his irritation and pulled his wallet out of his back pocket. He withdrew a card and handed it to the woman. "Please see that Mr. Feeney gets this card. He can call and reschedule when his calendar is less crowded."

"Will do," the girl said brightly. "Sure you don't want to volunteer to work for the campaign?"

"Yeah, I'm not very political." He'd been in the Marine Corps long enough to avoid politics like the plague. It just got in the way of doing his duty. He supposed now that he was a civilian again, it was time to start thinking about his civic responsibilities.

But not today.

He returned to his truck, wondering if Feeney would bother to get back to him. Probably not.

Mike would just have to follow up later.

He called Heller and told him about Feeney's no-show. "The girl at campaign headquarters said he was called away, but I have to wonder if that wasn't just an excuse to blow off the appointment."

"Maybe Feeney agreed to meet with you before he had a chance to talk to Craig Bearden."

"And then Bearden told him to cancel?"

"Politicians are careful to control the message," Heller said. "He may want to know more about you before his people answer your questions."

"I left my card. It'll tell him my name and who I work for."

"That might make it less likely he'll talk to you, not more," Heller warned. "What are you doing next?"

"I'm not going to quit, if that's what you're asking." Mike had a feeling Heller—and maybe Quinn and Cameron, too—had been testing him with this impromptu investigation at first. He suspected they hadn't been all that interested in finding out why Charlie Winters had decided to take his self-defense class. They were more interested in seeing how well Mike was able to investigate Charlie and her motives.

But that had been before someone had cut Charlie's brakes.

"By the way, Strong, Cameron wants a word with you tomorrow after your afternoon class. Can you drop by her office around five?"

"I'll be there." He ended the call and opened the calendar app to jot down the details of his appointment with Rebecca Cameron. Heller was an old friend from the Marine Corps, and Alexander Quinn, the wily spymaster who had been a legend during his time in the CIA, had crossed Mike's path from time to time during his tours of duty. But Cameron, a former diplomat, was a virtual stranger. She'd been an assistant to the American ambassador in Kaziristan during Mike's two years in that war-troubled country. But he'd met her only once, briefly, under difficult circumstances.

Why did she want to talk to him now? Was it something to do with what happened to Charlie?

THURSDAY AFTERNOON WAS cold and rainy, the mild warm snap of the first part of the week long gone. Forecasters were even talking about sleet and snow flurries for the weekend, driving out the last of Charlie's doubts about the wisdom of catching a ride with Mike to Campbell Cove Academy.

He arrived a half hour early, as promised. She thwarted any chivalrous instinct he might have had about getting out of the truck in the downpour by racing out the door the minute she heard the truck. Darting through the rain, she hauled herself into the passenger seat and turned to him with a laugh. "I now officially think catching a ride with you was a great idea."

He smiled back at her. "I thought you might."

"So, mind giving me a sneak preview of what we'll be doing in class today?" She shook the rain out of her hair and buckled in.

"The first part of the class won't be any different from what we've been doing in the beginner's class. Stretching is stretching."

"But afterward?"

He just smiled. "You'll see."

Even though Mike was able to find a parking place close to the gym entrance, they still were mostly drenched by the time they burst through the doors. Charlie ran her fingers through her wet hair, attempting to tame the curls trying to burst out all over. She could tell by Mike's amused glance that it was a lost cause.

"You can wait in the gym if you like. I've got a little paperwork to tackle in my office and a couple of phone calls to make before class. It would only bore you."

"That's fine." She gave a little wave as he walked out the side door of the gymnasium, quelling the urge to follow him.

She had done most of her stretching exercises by the time some of her other classmates started to drift into the gym. They greeted her with nods in the normal way of strangers thrown together by circumstance and, as she didn't encourage any further conversation, most settled in a few feet away on the floor mats to follow her lead and do their stretches.

By five minutes until class time, seven other students had entered, almost all of them male. She was also pretty sure most if not all of them were cops or some sort of law enforcement officers. Nobody survived life in her neck of the Kentucky woods without developing the ability to pick out a police officer in a crowd.

As she pushed to her feet, the door from outside opened, and one more student entered the gym, stopping in the doorway to survey the room, as if he expected trouble to break out any second.

His gaze locked with Charlie's, and she swallowed a groan.

Of all the people to run into here at the Campbell Cove Academy...

The newcomer was tall and well built, with broad shoulders and a lean waist that hadn't gained any padding since the last time Charlie had seen him almost ten years ago. His gray eyes were hard but sharp, like chips of flint, and his lips curved in a thin smile as he approached the mat where she stood.

"Well, if it isn't Charlotte Winters."

She hid her dismay with a smart-alecky grin in return. "Well, if it isn't Deputy Trask."

Archer Trask's smile widened, without a hint of humor making it anywhere near his eyes. "Have you woken up wasted in your backyard lately?"

Across the gym, the side door opened and Mike Strong walked through, his pace full of energy and purpose. His hair had dried during the time he'd spent in his office. In fact, he looked far more unruffled and put together than she felt at the moment.

Charlie turned away from Trask and moved closer to the other cops in the room. At least none of them looked familiar.

"Five more minutes," Mike called, taking his place at the front of the gym. He gave a little wave of his hand, and the rest of the class continued their stretching exercises.

Charlie continued with her stretches as well, hoping Archer Trask would go somewhere else and leave her alone.

In that, she was disappointed.

"So, how'd you end up here?" Trask's voice was deceptively casual.

"Here as in Campbell Cove?"

"No, here as in a self-defense course. Picked up a stalker or something?"

Charlie slanted a look at him, wondering for a moment if he'd heard about what happened to her car the previous day. "Only you, apparently."

"I heard you had a car accident yesterday."

So he *had* heard. "Is that the sort of thing people in your department investigate, Deputy Trask?"

"Not drinking *that* early, were you?"

She shot him a glare. "Go to hell."

"Something wrong here?"

At the sound of Mike's voice, both Charlie and Trask took a step back.

"Not a thing," Trask said, wandering away.

Mike moved closer to Charlie. "You look angry."

"I'm fine."

"Do you and Archer know each other?"

"Not really. Not in years." She made herself calm down. Getting into a fight with Archer Trask after all this time was the absolute *worst* thing she could do if she was serious about finding the truth about Alice's death. He'd been one of the first cops on the scene. She might end up needing his corroboration sooner or later.

Mike lowered his voice. "Has he been bothering you before today?"

She looked up sharply, realizing what he was asking. "No. No, of course not. Deputy Trask is just— No. This has nothing to do with what happened to my car. I promise you."

"You don't know who tampered with your car. How can you be so sure who it wasn't?"

"Trask is a cop. I'm a Winters. Around here, that's like oil and water."

Mike didn't appear appeased, but he gave a brief nod and turned to the rest of the class. "Okay, let's get started."

CHARLIE WAS QUIET on the drive back to her house, a stewing sort of silence that made Mike uneasy. She had managed to pull herself together after her run-in with Archer Trask, doing a creditable job of holding her own in the advanced self-defense class. She had a gangly, slightly awkward way of moving that reminded Mike of a long-legged puppy trying to figure out how to run, but what she lacked in pure grace she made up for in fierce intensity. She fought like a person who'd faced trouble before and would do anything to survive.

He broke the silence as they took the turn onto Sycamore Road. "You want to tell me about your history with Deputy Trask?"

She sent a glare angling his way. "No."

"Might make you feel better."

She laughed. "Trust me. It wouldn't."

He let it go. He had Archer Trask's contact information. If he wanted to know more about the deputy's relationship with Charlie, he could go to the source. "You did well today. Hung tough. Good job."

The look she gave him made him wonder if the concept of praise was foreign to her. "Thanks."

He pulled up at the curb in front of her house. "You want me to go inside with you?"

She shook her head. "No, I'm sure that's not necessary. Thanks for the ride. Hopefully, I'll have my car back by the next session."

She slipped out of the truck without saying anything further, loping up the flagstone walkway to her front porch. He waited, not wanting to leave until she was safely inside.

But she stopped with her hand on the doorknob, her body straightening suddenly. She turned to look at him. Even from several yards away, he saw the alarm in her expression.

He slid out of the truck and hurried up the walkway toward her. "What's wrong?"

She met him at the bottom of the steps, her eyes wide and scared. "I locked my door this afternoon before I left. Didn't I? You were here. You saw me do it, didn't you?"

He nodded.

"Well, it's not locked now."

He put his hand on her arm. "Wait here."

But she tagged along, right behind him, as he climbed the porch steps and approached the door.

She'd already touched the doorknob, so the likelihood that an intruder's prints were still intact was a long shot. But Mike used the hem of his T-shirt to turn the knob anyway, trying not to smudge anything.

He braced himself for the possibility of a blitz attack as he pushed the door open. His pistol was locked in the glove box of the truck. Too late to go back and get it now.

He stepped inside and swept the room, military style. There was no sign of an intruder still hanging around the living room.

But his handiwork was everywhere.

"Oh, my God." Behind him, Charlie's voice shook as she got a good look at the devastation.

Furniture was ripped apart and overturned. Picture frames had been smashed to the floor, scattering shards of glass across the hardwood. Porcelain knick-knacks had been crunched to dust underfoot, mixing with clouds of fiberfill from the ripped-up sofa cushions. A wood rocking chair lay on its side near the hearth, its rockers now perpendicular, the wood snapped almost in two.

"Who would do this?" Charlie moaned.

"You should go back outside," Mike said as he caught sight of something dark and wet amid the clumps of fiberfill. Something that looked like…

"Is that blood?" Charlie asked.

"I don't know—maybe?"

"Oh, God!" She rushed past him before he could stop her, disappearing into the back of the house.

He followed. "Charlie, wait!"

As he reached a room near the back of the house, Charlie's voice rose in a wordless wail.

He skidded to a stop in the open doorway, his heart in his throat.

Charlie knelt on the floor in front of a Siamese cat lying on its side, blood darkening his smoky fur.

Chapter Five

Charlie couldn't breathe. Her pulse hammered in her ears, deafening her, as she reached down to touch His Highness's dark fur. "Hizzy."

The cat's blue eyes opened, his head lifting at the sound of her voice. His blue eyes blinked slowly, his breath coming in little pants.

"Oh, baby, you're alive." Tamping down her panic, she made herself breathe, running her fingers over his body. The tremble in her fingers started to dissipate as she found the source of the blood. "He's got a wound in his shoulder. It's deep. But he's still alive." She looked at Mike over her shoulder.

He stared back at her, his brow furrowed and his eyes dark with an emotion she couldn't quite read.

"There are a couple of cat carriers in the mudroom at the back of the house," she told him. "Just to the left of the kitchen. Find those for me. And there should be dry towels in the bathroom. I'll need a couple of those, too."

She checked her watch. Almost six. But the staff at her vet's office didn't leave until six thirty, and she could call ahead, let them know there was an emergency case on the way.

"Nellie?" she called gently, hoping her nervous girl had stayed true to form and hidden somewhere the moment she realized there was a stranger in the house.

A plaintive mewling noise came from under the bed. Charlie scooted a few feet across the floor to the bed and looked underneath. Nellie's green eyes stared back at her, wide and afraid. "Are you okay, baby? Come out and let me take a look."

At the sound of Mike's footsteps coming down the hall, she called out, "Wait out there a minute."

Nellie froze, but Charlie made another coaxing sound. The tortoiseshell cat slinked from under the bed and rubbed her head against Charlie's shoulder.

Charlie gave the cat a quick check. She seemed uninjured. Charlie dropped her chin to her chest, trembling with relief.

"Charlie, can I come in yet?" Mike's soft voice sent Nellie scurrying back under the bed.

Charlie didn't try to coax her back out. "Yeah. Did you find the carriers?"

He entered the room, holding a towel and the two plastic carriers. "Why two of these?"

"I have a second cat, but she's okay. She's hiding under the bed." Charlie took the towel from Mike and gently wrapped it around Hizzy's bloodstained body, wincing as the cat uttered a low yowl of pain. "It's okay, sweetie. We're going to get you some help."

Mike crouched by her and set the carrier on the floor. "What can I do?"

"Open the carrier door and hold it until I can get him inside."

Mike did as she asked, and she eased His Highness into the portable cage, trying not to let panic take over again, despite how scary she found it that the cat wasn't fighting her at all. Usually, getting His Highness into the carrier was a battle of wills.

She snapped the door shut. "I hate leaving Nellie here, in case someone comes back."

"I've called someone from the agency to guard your house while we're gone."

She looked up at him, surprised. "Someone from your agency?"

"Yeah. Technically, this is a crime scene. You should call it in to the cops."

Her knee-jerk reaction was to shake her head no.

"Charlie, someone cut your brakes yesterday. Today, they trashed your house and injured your cat. Call the police."

"There's no time. We need to get Hizzy to the vet. In fact, I need to call ahead to make sure the doctor stays around." As Mike picked up the carrier, she led the way, pulling her phone from her pocket. She dialed the number, holding her breath until someone answered. As she and Mike hurried for the truck, she summarized the situation for the vet clinic assistant, who assured her the doctor would be waiting.

"Eric Brannon is on his way here." Mike buckled up and started the truck. "You need to call the police."

She sighed, aware he was right. "It's not an emergency, so I don't want to call 911."

"I have Deputy Trask's phone number in my phone," Mike murmured.

She looked at him. "No."

"So there *is* some bad blood between you two."

She waved toward the right when they reached the four-way stop. "The vet clinic is a half mile down this road, on the left."

In her lap, cradled by the carrier, His Highness had stopped his heavy panting, giving her a moment's panic. But when she looked into the carrier's metal grid door, Hizzy blinked back at her. His breathing had returned to something approaching normal, she realized, starting to feel a little more hopeful.

The doctor himself, Pete Terrell, greeted them at the door. He was a thick-set, bearded man in jeans and a blue plaid flannel shirt under a white coat, with a friendly, competent manner that made Charlie feel instantly better about His Highness's chances of survival.

"I'll wait out here and check to see what's going on with Eric," Mike said, pulling out his cell phone. "Is it okay if I call the cops, as well?"

Charlie's gaze flicked between him and the vet. "Yes. But not Trask."

She followed Dr. Terrell into the exam room and set the carrier on the table. "I found him on the floor. He was bleeding from his upper left torso, around his shoulder. There seems to be a deep laceration there, but I didn't see any other wounds."

"All right, big fella. Let's take a look." Dr. Terrell gently eased the cat from the carrier and unfolded the towel holding him still. Blood had seeped into the terry cloth of the towel, but not a lot, she was heartened to see.

She held His Highness by his back legs, but the cat wasn't kicking up his usual fuss. He seemed to know he was in need of help and didn't try to fight.

A scrubs-clad veterinary assistant came into the room. She nodded at Charlie and took her place with His Highness so Charlie could step back and observe.

"We've got a laceration in the vicinity of the left scapula," the doctor murmured. "Deep. To the bone. Margins are clean and uniform. I'd say it's a knife wound. Smooth blade."

Charlie pressed her hands to her face, feeling sick at the thought.

"It isn't that wide. Looks like a stab rather than a slash." The doctor looked up at her. "What happened?"

"I don't know," she admitted. "I got home from an appointment and my place was trashed. Furniture ripped up, things shattered and crushed. And then I saw blood and followed the trail to Hizzy."

"He's a lucky cat. It looks as if the blade hit the scapula and bounced off before it hit any internal organs. I'm going to want X-rays to be sure."

"Of course."

A half hour later, the doctor had stitched Hizzy up and transferred him to a cage, hooked up to an IV drip. "To replenish the fluids he lost from bleeding," Dr. Terrell explained. "We'll want to keep him overnight for observation, but I think he'll be okay. Barring any unexpected complications, you can probably take him home tomorrow."

Charlie blinked back tears of relief. "Are you sure?"

"He was a little shocky when he came in, but his vitals have stabilized nicely. He's young and otherwise healthy, and you got him here quickly." Dr. Terrell patted her shoulder. "How about Nellie? I take it she wasn't injured?"

"She's fine. Scared and hiding, but fine."

"I hope you find out who did this." Dr. Terrell's smiling demeanor slipped. "You know, it's possible His Highness in there scratched whoever stabbed him. I could clip his claw tips and save them for you. Might be some DNA on them."

She stared at him, unable to stop a wobbly smile. "DNA on a cat's claws. I never even thought of that."

She returned to the vet clinic waiting room to find Mike sitting on one of the benches, scrolling through his phone. He looked up quickly, his brow furrowed when he realized she wasn't holding the cat carrier. "What happened?" he asked, his tone cautious.

"He's going to be okay, but they want to keep him overnight for observation. You know, pump some fluid into him, keep him lightly sedated for pain. The doctor said I'll probably be able to take him home tomorrow."

Mike's worried expression cleared. "That's great news. You ready to go, then?"

She glanced back toward the hall that led to the overnight cages. "As ready as I'll ever be."

In the truck, Mike told her there were policemen at the house waiting for her. "I mentioned what happened with your brakes yesterday."

She grimaced. "I wish you hadn't done that."

"I figured you'd say that."

"So you told them anyway, knowing I'd object?"

He glanced at her. "This is serious. The brake line alone could have been an accident. But a break-in and the intentional injury to your cat—"

"Dr. Terrell thinks Hizzy might have scratched the person who stabbed him."

"Can they clip his claws for DNA?"

Charlie gave a small huff of grim laughter. "Yeah. It's already in the works."

"Brannon waited outside your house for the cops. We agreed it was smart to leave the scene as it was for the police."

"It was a break-in. Cops barely blink at break-ins."

"It was a break-in with injury."

She stared at him. "Injury to a cat. That's not exactly going to warrant a task force around here. The cops have enough real crimes to investigate—drug trafficking, murder, fraud…"

"The cops can do whatever they're going to do. But I'm treating this like the threat it was obviously meant to be."

Something in Mike's tone sent a little quiver up her spine. "What do you mean?"

"If the police won't take your safety seriously, I will."

She stared at him for a moment, struggling for a response. "Why would you do that?"

"Because protecting people is what I do."

"For pay. And I can't pay you anything. I don't make that kind of money."

"I'm not asking for pay."

"You do realize that makes no sense, don't you?"

They had reached Charlie's house. A single Campbell Cove Police Department cruiser sat parked in the driveway, while a silver sedan sat at the curb. "That's Eric's car," Mike said, nodding at the sedan.

Brannon was still on the porch. He stood and walked down the flagstone path to greet them. "Officer Bentley is photographing the destruction in your house," he told Charlie. "He'll want you to take a look around when he's done, to see if anything has been stolen."

Her laptop, she thought with a sudden rush of panic. In the chaos of dealing with Hizzy's injury, she'd forgotten all about her computer. Beyond all her work files—absolutely vital for her job—there were the files she'd started to compile of her research into what had happened the night Alice died.

All of those files were backed up to a cloud archive, so she wouldn't lose anything. And the security on her laptop was top-notch. It wouldn't be easy to crack her passwords.

But if the wrong person got his hands on those

research files about Alice, they'd know how much she knew.

And how much she didn't.

She entered the house, trying to control her rising panic. Ignoring the sounds of the police officer moving around in her kitchen at the back of the house, she hurried into her bedroom.

The laptop was where she'd left it.

With a sigh of relief, she dropped into the desk chair and opened the lid. The machine flickered to life, the lock screen greeting her.

She typed in the password to unlock the system and started scrolling through her files, checking to see if there was any sign of an intrusion.

Everything seemed to be the way she'd left it. As far as she could tell, no one had accessed her Alice Bearden files since she'd last had them open the day before.

"This is still a crime scene, Charlie." The twangy drawl that made her whirl around belonged to a barrel-chested cop with a weathered face and a crooked smile.

"Officer Everett." Charlie stood up. "I know. I just— I work from this computer, and if someone had gotten in her and messed things up—"

Bob Everett's smile widened. "Lord, look at you, girl. All growed up. How's your mama?"

Bob had always been a little sweet on Charlie's mother, she remembered. They'd been schoolmates years earlier, and apparently Bob had never quite lost his soft spot for Marlene.

"She's doing pretty good these days," Charlie said.

It was mostly true. Marlene had been married to her new husband for almost four years. "She's in Arkansas now. With her new husband."

"Yeah." Bob's expression fell.

She changed the subject to put him out of his misery. "I guess you want to know if anything's been stolen."

"Well, I've been taking a good look around. Everything's an unholy mess, but the kind of stuff you figure a burglar's gonna take seems to all be here. Your TV, your stereo system, your computer. The TV and stereo are all busted up, but they're still here."

But they hadn't done anything to her computer, she thought. Maybe because they wanted to access the files within?

But why hadn't they just stolen the laptop while they had the chance?

"Is the destruction throughout the house?" she asked.

"Looks like they stopped here. Didn't see nothing out of place in the kitchen or the mudroom, and the next room down doesn't look like it's been touched, either."

The only damage in the bedroom was Hizzy's blood on the hardwood floor. They hadn't done the sort of destruction here they'd done in the front of the house.

"Maybe someone interrupted them?"

Charlie and Bob both looked up at the sound of Mike's voice. He stood in the bedroom doorway, his broad shoulders filling the space.

"Who are you?" Bob asked.

"Mike Strong. I'm a friend of Charlie's."

Bob looked from Charlie to Mike and back, his expression skeptical. "Well, Mr. Strong, I guess it's possible the intruders got interrupted. I'll talk to the neighbors and see if anyone saw or heard anything. But I don't know there's much more I can do here. I could call in a crew to do fingerprints, Charlie, but I gotta be honest. If they didn't steal anything, and you don't reckon they did, what you're lookin' at here is plain ol' vandalism. You'd be better off callin' your insurance company and lettin' them handle the claim."

Charlie looked at Mike. He sighed and looked away.

"I appreciate your comin' by, Officer Everett." She walked with him to the door.

Bob turned in the doorway, his expression darkening. "I heard they hurt one of your cats. I hope the little fella's gonna be okay."

"Doc Terrell seems to think so."

"Good to hear. You let me know if anything else happens, you hear?"

"Thanks. I will. And I meant what I said about Mama. I bet she'd love you to drop by and say hello."

Bob smiled at her again, looking ridiculously pleased. "I'll do that."

She watched him go, swallowing a sigh.

"You were right. The cops aren't going to be able to protect you." Mike's voice was close behind her.

She turned to look at him. "I know. I'll get better

locks. Maybe splurge on a security system. I just never thought I'd need one here."

"You can't stay here alone. Especially without a car."

"I'll be fine. I don't think they'll be coming back so soon."

He put his hands on her shoulders, his grip somehow both gentle and firm. "Charlie, look at this place." He turned her until she faced the chaos that the intruder had made of her once-tidy living room. The sight of her stereo system lying shattered on the floor brought tears stinging to her eyes. She'd bought the system on her twenty-first birthday, after saving up every penny she could during her four years of college. It had been the first thing to ever truly belong only to her, and she'd spent the past eight years enjoying the thing, even as it aged and, in the eyes of a lot of people, grew obsolete.

She blinked back the tears. "I saw it before."

"This isn't just vandalism. This is terrorism."

She twisted her head to look at him. "Terrorism?"

"Terrorism is more than just bombs in Baghdad or Jerusalem, Charlie. It can be graffiti painted on the wall of a black man's home or a Jewish man's shop. It can be stalkers sending threatening notes to their prey. This—" He waved his hand at the mess. "This is meant to terrorize you."

"Well, it won't work," she said firmly.

"Good. But you can't just declare it won't work and then go on with your life the way it is."

"If I change my life, doesn't that mean the terrorists

win?" She meant the question to be flip and breezy, but to her own surprise, it came out angry.

He reached up and brushed away a lock of hair that had flopped into her face. His fingertips brushed down her cheek before he dropped his hand to his side. "I'm not asking you to change your life. I'm just offering to watch your back."

"Why?" The sensation of his touch lingered on her skin. She tried to ignore it, struggling to focus.

"Because I hate terrorists," he said simply.

"Oh."

"I'll stay here tonight."

No. That was a bad idea.

Wasn't it?

"There's no sofa left," she said, her voice faint.

"I'll sleep on the floor in the spare room. I've got a rucksack in my truck's lockbox that has some camping gear."

"I can't pay you," she reminded him.

"This is a freebie." His lopsided smile made her heart flip in response. "I'll go talk to Eric and then I'll be right back. We can tackle some of this mess tonight if you like, or we can wait until morning."

Oh, what the hell, she thought. She could certainly use his help cleaning up the place. And if he wanted to spend the night on her hardwood floor, roughing it, who was she to say no?

The truth was, she'd feel a lot safer with him here.

She sighed. "I'd be stupid to say no, wouldn't I?"

"And stupid," he said softly, "is something you're not."

She watched him go, thinking with every step he took that she should call him back, change her mind. Tell him to go home. She'd be fine. She didn't need him watching her back.

But somehow, he was out the door before she opened her mouth.

Releasing a shaky breath, she looked around the living room, taking in the malicious destruction, and couldn't muster up any regret for having agreed that he could stay the night.

The last thing she wanted right now was to be alone.

Chapter Six

"She's playing it tough and stoic, but I know she's got to be scared." Mike glanced toward the front door of Charlie's house, remembering the look on her face when she'd seen the blood on the floor. "Brake tampering yesterday, and now this."

"And she doesn't have any idea who could be behind either of these attacks?" Eric's breath fogged in the cold night air.

"She says not. I'm not sure I believe her."

"You're staying with her tonight?"

"Yeah, unless she changes her mind and kicks me out."

"And if she does?"

"I'll stay in my truck and watch the place from there."

Eric nodded slowly, not saying anything for a moment. Finally, he looked up at Mike, his blue eyes gleaming in the faint moonlight peeking through the scudding clouds overhead. "You really do think she's in trouble, don't you?"

"I do." Mike rubbed his chin, his beard stubble

scraping against his palm. "There's something in her past—I can't really talk about it, but it's reason to worry."

"Something she did?"

"Maybe. I don't know. Something she was involved in, a long time ago. Someone died, and I don't know how exactly she was involved, but it's a place to start looking."

"Did the intruders take anything?"

"Charlie says no."

"So they just made that awful mess for the hell of it?"

"Or maybe as a warning," Mike said.

Eric pressed his lips into a tight line. "Stabbed the cat for the same reason?"

"Maybe. Or maybe the cat got in the way. Wrong place at the wrong time."

"Hissing and spitting, getting in the way…"

"Right."

Eric's voice dipped a notch. "Do the bosses know you're getting involved in Charlie's mess?"

"Sort of." Mike hadn't really talked to Heller about anything that had happened since the tampered brakes incident. His boss was probably expecting to hear something from him soon. "I'll give Heller a call. Catch him up on everything."

But not tonight. He couldn't risk Heller telling him to back off and let Charlie handle things alone.

He didn't want to defy a direct order.

"You want me to stick around awhile?" Eric asked. "I could help with the cleanup."

Mike thought about it. "I think she's going to be uncomfortable enough with me there. You go on home. If anything comes up, I have your number."

Eric clapped him on the shoulder. "Okay. Take care. Tell Charlie I'm sorry about the mess, and I hope her cat's going to be okay."

When Mike entered the house, he found Charlie already hard at work cleaning up the mess. She had a broom and a long-handled dustpan in her hands, sweeping up the shattered bits of her belongings and dumping them into a large trash can lined with a plastic bin liner.

"How can I help?" he asked.

She looked up at him, her hazel eyes dark with anger, and for a second, he feared she was going to throw him out. But finally, she thrust the dustpan at him. "I'll sweep. You dump."

He took the dustpan and helped her sweep up the mess. When the worst of the small pieces had been thrown away, they started tackling the bigger pieces of detritus—the ruined sofa cushions, the mangled bits of electronics. They worked that way for another hour, in silent concert, until the living room had been cleared of most of the chaos.

"Good thing someone scared them off," Charlie muttered as she retrieved the dustpan from him. "Or we might have been at this all night."

"Why don't you go on to bed?" he suggested. "I can lock up."

"Fat lot of good that lock did me today," she muttered, slanting an accusing glare at the door.

"We'll put in a new lock tomorrow. And if you're serious about a security system, that's one of the things we offer at Campbell Cove Security Services."

She turned her glare on him. "So all this solicitude is a sales pitch?"

"No, of course not—"

She gave his arm a light punch and grinned. "Just kidding."

He couldn't muster up a smile in return. "You *are* taking this stuff seriously, aren't you, Charlie?"

Her smile faded. "Yeah, I'm taking it seriously. I just don't know why it's happening."

"Are you sure about that?"

Her eyes narrowed. "Believe me, if I knew who was doing this, I'd find a way to stop it myself."

He moved away from her, crossing to the remains of a rocker they'd stacked next to the door. He'd told her not to throw it out until he'd had a chance to look at it more closely. He crouched next to it now, examining the damage. "It's just— It seems such a coincidence that you start taking a self-defense class and suddenly you're facing two threatening incidents."

"Coincidence. Luck. Whatever you want to call it." She didn't sound terribly convincing.

He quelled the urge to look at her and kept his focus on the rocking chair instead. The pieces weren't broken, he realized with a closer look. The legs were pulled out of their sockets and the rockers twisted out of place, but none of the individual pieces had been damaged. He could put everything back together with a little wood glue and elbow grease. "Okay. Whatever you say."

"You make it sound as if you think I'm lying."

He stood and turned slowly to face her. "I think I can fix that rocker, no problem."

Her lips thinned with annoyance, and she took a couple of belligerent steps toward him. "You *do* think I'm lying. Don't you?"

"Yeah. I do. But it's your business. I could do a better job of helping you protect yourself if you'd level with me, but that's entirely up to you. I'll do what I can. The rest is up to you."

Her nostrils flared, and he could tell she was furious, but he had a feeling she was angrier with herself than with him.

"I'm going to bed," she said bluntly and walked out of the room.

He watched her go, wondering how long it would take her to realize she couldn't face her trouble alone.

ALICE'S SMILE WAS ELECTRIC, her straight white teeth gleaming in the bluish tint of the bar's low light. "Relax, Charlie. Nobody here knows us. And it's just beer, right?"

Her stomach was already cramping with anxiety. If her mother found out what she'd been doing, she'd freak completely. Charlie was supposed to be the sane one in the family. These days, with Vernon and Jamie up in Blackburn Prison, and the other two boys barely keeping their noses clean, Mama depended on Charlie to be the one she didn't have to worry about.

And here she was, three years under the legal drinking age, at one of the seediest bars in eastern Kentucky, nursing a light beer and hoping like hell nobody she knew walked into the place.

"Isn't this place great?" Alice sipped her Trouble Maker through a long black straw, her blue eyes shimmering with excitement. "This is a big night, Charlie. Bigger than you know."

"Why?" Charlie asked.

Alice's gaze flitted around the room, never settling anywhere, though for a moment, when her lips curved around the straw, Charlie thought Alice might have spotted someone she knew. But when Charlie twisted around to see what Alice was looking at, all she saw was a stuffy-looking man in a shirt and tie, drinking something gold in a tumbler with ice. Whiskey of some sort. Probably bourbon.

"Do you know that guy?" Charlie asked.

Alice shook her head and took another sip of her cocktail. "Drink your beer, Charlie. It's just beer."

Charlie took a sip of the beer, grimaced at the bitter, yeasty taste and wished she'd gone for something like red wine instead. At least it would have been sweet. And classy.

Instead, she was sitting here in her short ill-fitting dress, drinking a low-rent beer like the low-rent little redneck she was.

Alice had flitted away, her womanly curves selling the lie that she was over twenty-one. Red was her color, and she was wearing the hell out of the body-skimming little red dress with the tiny spaghetti straps and the hem that stopped several inches above her knees. Her tawny blond hair was scooped up into a messy ponytail, with lots of wavy golden tendrils dancing around her face and neck as she walked.

The room was starting to feel close and hot, and her stomach was rumbling a little. Maybe she should have eaten something before coming here, but she'd been too nervous and jittery to swallow even a bite of the sandwich she'd made before leaving the house.

She should relax. Try to have fun.

She took a third sip of the beer. It didn't taste any better than the first two sips. The rumbling in her stomach continued, accompanied by a cold sweat breaking out on her forehead.

The room closed in on her. The lights seemed to dance before her eyes in rhythm with the bass beat of the music blaring from the music speakers. She pushed away from the bar, leaving the beer where it sat. She wasn't going to drink any more of it, especially not the way her stomach felt.

There was an outdoor patio. She could see other bar patrons out there, enjoying the unseasonably mild night. She slipped her leather jacket on, gave her skirt a quick downward tug and weaved her way through the crowd.

The air outside was colder than she'd expected, but she didn't mind. In fact, the chilly night air seemed to clear her foggy brain for a moment.

But then the dizzy sensation returned, along with a sudden, bone-deep weariness. She found an empty table near the edge of the porch and sat, pressing her hands to her eyes.

"There she is." The voice was male. Distant. Sort of familiar, though Charlie couldn't place it.

"How much longer?" That whisper was female, and for a confused moment, Charlie was sure it was Alice's voice.

"Soon, I think," the male voice answered, closer now.

Charlie put her head on the table, closing her eyes against the whirl of color and light assaulting her brain.

Then it all went away. For what felt like a long time.

The darkness ebbed slowly, replaced by a muddy yellow glow just beyond her closed eyelids. Something hard, cold and damp lay beneath Charlie's cheek. It smelled of gasoline and grime, and as she tried to move her head, grit stung against her skin.

She stopped trying to move and concentrated instead on opening her eyes. Her eyelids felt leaded, hard to lift. She forced them open anyway.

The light came from streetlamps. Without moving her head, she couldn't see the lamps themselves, but the circular glow that spilled onto the pavement suggested the light source.

Something lay in the street a few feet away from her. Red and pale white. Crumpled. Still. The tawny waves spilled out around her head, streaked with blood. One blue eye was open and staring.

Alice. Oh, God, Alice!

The world seemed to narrow to a pinpoint, until all she could see in the blackness was that one blue eye.

Then it disappeared into an endless black void.

Charlie fought against the darkness, but she couldn't seem to move. Couldn't push air past her vocal cords to make a sound.

She wanted to scream her fear and anguish. Cry out for help. Beg for someone to find them and save them from whatever had happened.

But she couldn't.

Hands caught her arms and gave her a shake, and she heard a voice in the blackness.

"Charlie!"

CHARLIE JERKED AWAKE, her breath rising on a keening gasp. For a moment, she felt as if she was still trapped in the darkness, but after a panicked few seconds, the dim light from outside the house filtered through the curtains and into her sightless eyes, and she realized she was in her own bed, in the small house on Sycamore Road.

And the strong hands clutching her shoulders belonged to the broad-shouldered man sitting on the bed beside her.

"Charlie?" He sounded wary.

She realized her hands were bunched into fists in front of her, pushing against Mike's hard chest. His hard, bare chest.

She dropped them to her lap. "Sorry. I must have been dreaming."

"You called out a name," he said quietly.

"I did?" She shook her head, not sure she wanted to remember whatever images fluttered elusively at the edge of her mind.

"You called out the name Alice," he said. "Does that mean anything to you?"

"Yes."

He waited a moment, perhaps expecting her to continue. When she didn't, he added, "You sounded scared."

The image from the dream had stuck with her, vivid in a way dreams rarely were once she awoke. She could see Alice lying crumpled in the wet street, her hair splayed around her head. She could see the blood staining Alice's tawny hair and the blank stare of her one visible eye.

She'd never remembered seeing Alice before. The voices, the jumble of words and phrases that had played games with her mind, yes. But the sight of Alice, lying dead in the road—that image was new.

Was it a memory? Or was it her vibrant imagination bringing Alice's death to life for her?

She didn't know. She only knew that something wasn't right. She had taken three sips of light beer and her head had started to swim. She wasn't much of a drinker, but she knew that it would take a lot more than three sips of beer to make the world turn upside down the way it had.

And no way would it have made the rest of the night a blank until she woke in her own backyard just before dawn the next morning.

"What are you thinking?" Mike asked.

She shook her head, not ready to share her thoughts with someone she'd just met. Not until she'd had a chance to try to piece everything she was starting to remember together into a more coherent pattern.

The last thing she needed to do was give people ammunition to dismiss her stories as typical Charlie Winters's confabulation.

"I was just trying to remember my dream," she said. That answer was true, wasn't it? If not quite complete.

"And did you?"

"Bits and pieces." She pressed her hands to her face. Her elbow brushed against Mike's arm, reminding her again just how close he was sitting to her.

And how little clothing he was wearing.

"What time is it?" she asked. She didn't have an alarm clock. She'd always lived by her own internal clock, somehow able to wake up in time to do whatever she needed to do.

"A little after three."

"And you heard me calling out from the living room?" That was where he'd bedded down for the night.

He shifted, running one hand through his short-cropped hair. "I moved the sleeping bag to the hall. Outside your door."

"Why?"

"Because I wasn't sure I could beat an intruder to your room if they entered through the back door."

"Oh." Clearly, he was taking the possibility of a threat against her life seriously. "I wish I could offer you a sofa to sleep on instead. Sleeping on a hard floor can't be fun."

His soft laugh was a warm, low grumble in the darkness. "Beats the hell out of sleeping on an Afghanistan mountainside in winter."

She jumped at the chance to change the subject. "How long were you in Afghanistan?"

"A couple of years. I went to Afghanistan first, then Iraq. Then Kaziristan for a few years."

"Then where?"

His tone grew suddenly cautious. "Then I retired and came back to the States."

"How long ago was that?"

"A couple of years. I worked security here and there for a little over a year before one of my bosses called to see if I was interested in working for him at Campbell Cove Academy. He was looking for instructors and thought I'd be good for the job."

"You seem pretty good at it," she said. "Not that I have a lot of experience with self-defense instructors."

"I'm just sharing some of the things I learned in boot camp. Geared toward civilians, of course."

"Yeah, no rifles or bayonets in our training."

"Well, not at the intermediate level, no."

Her eyes must have better adjusted to the dark, because she could see the pale white gleam of his teeth in the dark, suggesting he'd spoken the last words with a smile.

"Why did the security company choose little Campbell Cove, Kentucky, as their home base?" she asked, starting to enjoy the warm intimacy of the moonlit conversation.

"Not sure," he admitted. "I think maybe one of the owners is from this area. I know they liked the seclusion of the property. It's not easy to get to if you don't live right in the area. And we're in a place where we can see trouble coming well ahead of time."

She nodded, only half listening to his words. Instead, she was drinking in his voice, a gravelly rumble of masculinity that somehow made this dark bedroom feel like the safest place on earth.

"I like it here," he added. "It reminds me of home."

"And where's home?" she asked, feeling half-drunk from his nearness.

"North Carolina."

"Whereabouts?"

"I lived a little ways east of Cherokee, in the Smokies. A town called Black Rock."

"Evocative."

"Yeah?"

She closed her eyes, breathing deeply. In the warmth that flowed between them, she could smell a faint piney scent coming from him. It reminded her of long, hot summers playing in the mountain woodlands as a child, as perfect a memory as she had.

"I can picture the place. It's small. Surrounded by the woods and mountains. There's probably a little creek running through the town, and a little stretch of downtown you can drive through in about a minute. Am I close?"

"Yeah, pretty close," he admitted. "You sure you've never been there?"

"Yes." She opened her eyes. He was looking at her, his gaze intense, as if he could read her expression in the dark. "I'm just from a place a lot like that. Bagwell, Kentucky. Population six hundred and holding."

"I think I've been through there. It's on the way to Pineville, right?"

"Yeah."

Silence fell between them then, thick with exquisite tension. Attraction, she realized. Unsurprising on her part—he was talk, dark and lean, with the sort of powerful body that women bought magazines to drool over. His face looked as if it had been chiseled by a master sculptor, and that voice was made for seduction.

What threw her off balance, however, was the attraction she felt radiating from Mike. Attraction for her.

So not what she expected.

"You should try to go back to sleep," he said, rising from the bed and edging toward the door.

She felt his sudden absence keenly, as if a cold breeze had just washed over her. "Okay."

"Sweet dreams this time, okay?"

"I'll try," she said, grimacing a little at the smitten sound of her own voice. "You, too."

"'Night." He slipped from the room and closed the door.

Charlie laid her head back on her pillows and stared at the ceiling, about as far from sleep as she'd ever been.

Chapter Seven

"It had definitely been cut. Our forensics guys are trying to figure out what kind of blade made it."

Mike opened the refrigerator door and peered inside. Thank goodness the intruders hadn't made it as far as the kitchen. The carton of eggs stored in the door compartment was still intact. "Even if you do," he said into the phone, "we'd have to find a weapon before we could make a match, wouldn't we?"

"Probably," Maddox Heller admitted. "But maybe we can narrow down the type of blade. Then you can ask Charlie Winters if the description rings any bells."

"Yeah," he said, not adding that he couldn't be sure Charlie would tell him if she did find the description familiar. She was clearly keeping secrets from him, if her nightmare the night before was any indication.

"I take it there weren't any further problems last night?"

"No, it was quiet as a church." He'd already made a circuit of the house, indoors and out, to be sure there had been no further attempted incursions into Charlie's house. He supposed his big F-150 pickup parked in the driveway might have been enough to discourage the intruders from trying again.

He was curious, however, why they had stopped their destruction halfway through the house. The vandalism had obviously been meant as a warning of some sort. Had they figured one room's worth of destruction was enough? Or had something scared them off?

"I don't suppose the police bothered to ask the neighbors anything about the break-in," he said.

"I have a friend on the force. I can ask."

"Thanks. I'd appreciate that."

"By the way, Cameron still wants to see you."

He jerked upright, nearly hitting his head on the edge of the freezer door. "Oh, damn. I was supposed to meet with her yesterday afternoon."

"I told her what happened. She understood. But she says she still needs to see you, today if possible."

Footsteps padded softly down the hall toward the kitchen. "I'll call her and set something up," he said. "Gotta go."

He didn't wait for Heller to respond, pocketing his phone and turning to look at Charlie as she entered the kitchen.

She was still wearing the thermal pajamas she'd put on last night after showering before bed, the hem of the top scrunched up enough that he got a glimpse of flat stomach and the glint of a small silver belly ring. Her short hair was a spiky, bed-headed mess, and her hazel-green eyes drooped with weariness. "Coffee," she groaned.

He picked up the mug he'd set out for her, a dark green mug with the words *First Coffee, Then Coherence* on the front, and poured her a cup of the coffee he'd just brewed. "How do you like it?"

"Hot and now." She took the cup and swallowed a gulp, grimacing as it went down. But she took another gulp and leaned against the counter, looking at him beneath sleepy eyelids. "How long have you been up?"

He glanced at his watch. Seven thirty. "About an hour or so. Did I wake you?"

"No, my internal clock did that." She took another drink of the coffee. "No new intrusions, I take it?"

"Not that I saw." He turned back to the fridge. "Are you a breakfast-eater?"

"Yes, please. Are you cooking?" Her expression perked up. "Tell me you're cooking."

"I'm cooking, if you can settle for scrambled eggs."

"I'd settle for dry cereal, so eggs sound great." She poured a second cup of coffee, this time adding a packet of sweetener and a spoonful of the hazelnut creamer that sat in a plastic container next to the coffeepot. She fetched a spoon from a drawer and stirred the coffee as she crossed to the small table next to the kitchen window. Morning sunlight filtered through the pale blue curtains, bathing her pale face with a rosy glow.

"What time do you have to go to work?" Mike asked.

"Well, I usually like to be at the computer by eight thirty, since that's when the on-site staff shows up."

Mike frowned. "You work from home?"

She cocked her head. "I told you I had a flexible work schedule."

"Yeah, but I didn't connect that to working at home."

She set the coffee cup in front of her. "You seem... dismayed?"

"Well, I was thinking there'd be safety in numbers if you were going to an office somewhere." He carried three eggs to the stove and looked for a frying pan. "Where's the skillet?"

"Over the stove."

He found the pan and set it on the stove eye, setting the heat to medium high. "Do you use the laptop in your bedroom for work, or do you have a different computer?"

"I use the laptop," she answered, grabbing her cup and walking over to stand beside him. "You're really worried about my being here alone, aren't you?"

"Aren't you?"

She seemed to give the question some thought. "I wasn't. I figured these people don't want to risk getting caught, so they wouldn't attack me in my own home."

"But they were willing to kill you in your car."

"Or maybe they figured I'd think there was something wrong with the brakes before it became dangerous. If I hadn't been traveling on that particular road heading down a mountain, I wouldn't have had nearly as much trouble stopping my car, even without the brakes."

Heat radiated from the pan on the stove eye in front of him. He poured a dollop of oil into the pan and it sizzled immediately. He forced himself to concentrate on cooking for a few moments, until he was ready to spoon the fluffy yellow scrambled eggs onto the two plates Charlie had retrieved from a nearby cabinet.

She'd also put a couple of pieces of bread in the toaster. They popped up as he was spooning the eggs onto the plates. "Butter?"

"Sure," he answered. He'd hauled and tugged enough debris the night before while cleaning up Charlie's living room to allow himself the indulgence.

Over breakfast, he picked up the dropped thread of conversation. "I don't think you can assume the tampering with your brakes was just an attempt to frighten you."

"You're a very comforting man," she said drily.

"I'm serious, Charlie. Someone went to pretty drastic measures to put you in danger. And what happened in this house yesterday afternoon may have been just a warning, but it was a pretty brutal one."

"I'm taking it seriously." She put down her fork. "Believe me."

"I'm not crazy about leaving you here alone today." Mike poked at his eggs, not nearly as hungry now as he'd been a few minutes earlier. "Is there any way you could work from another location? Since you work on a laptop anyway."

"I could," she said with a slight nod, picking up her fork. She tried a bite of eggs. "Pretty good."

"Thanks."

"But there aren't any trendy little internet cafés anywhere around here," she added with a sigh. "And if I go over to Mercerville to the office, they may decide they like having me around there all the time."

"And that would be bad?"

"Very." She stuck out her chin. "One of the reasons I took this particular job was that I could work from home and keep flexible hours."

"Then come to my office."

She shook her head. "I can't leave this place. I can't. I have one traumatized cat still hiding under my bed and another I have to pick up from the vet today who's probably going to have to have one of those plastic cones around his head for the next few days. I can't leave them here alone, and I can't take them with me to your office."

"Then you can take them to my place."

His words fell like a bomb in the middle of the room. Charlie stared at him as if he'd lost his mind, and his own gut clenched as if he'd just taken a sucker punch.

"That is…an unexpected offer," Charlie said finally into the deafening silence.

"Yeah." He picked up his fork and poked at his eggs, now growing cold. "Kind of surprised myself with it, too."

"I won't hold you to it."

He dropped his fork. "I'm not saying it's a bad idea, Charlie."

"Moving into your place with my two special-needs cats isn't a bad idea?" Her expression oozed skepticism.

"No, listen," he said, starting to warm to the idea. "My place has good locks and a state-of-the-art security system. I have two bedrooms, which means I wouldn't have to sleep on the floor. Cable TV, Wi-Fi, central heat and air—"

"Are you trying to sell me on the idea or on a time-share?"

He smiled. "It could work, Charlie. I live close to the office, so if there was any kind of trouble, I could be there in minutes. It's right near the center of town in Mercerville, easy walking distance from a couple of eating places and shops. And I like cats."

"Even crazy ones?"

"Crazy is my favorite breed," he said. Of people as well as cats.

She sighed, her head cocking to one side as she considered it. "Cats can be messy. And temperamental."

"I grew up with cats. I'm not new at it."

"I can also be messy and temperamental."

"I'll cope." Was he really sitting here trying to talk her into invading his bachelor territory? After nearly ten years in the Marine Corps, living alone had turned out to be an unexpected pleasure. Not having to account to anyone else for what music he listened to, what television shows or movies he watched, how late he stayed up or how early he rose—why was he suddenly so eager to bring this unpredictable redhead and her two cats into his domain?

"Okay," she said.

"Okay," he echoed with a nod, wondering what the hell he'd just gotten himself into.

CHARLIE PULLED THE rolling chair closer to the wide oak desk where her laptop computer sat, trying to settle in. It wasn't that the chair itself was uncomfortable. It was the very opposite, a large, ergonomically built manager's chair with plush leather upholstery and caster wheels that moved as smoothly as a hot knife through butter.

No, the problem was the unfamiliarity of the setting and her own growing uneasiness at how quickly she'd allowed Mike to talk her into moving herself and the cats into his house.

What she needed, she realized, was a best friend. Someone like Alice, who'd understood her and could give her sound advice. The problem was, after Alice died, Charlie hadn't tried to find a new best friend. Best friends meant opening yourself up to loss and pain, and she'd had about all she could take of that, thank you very much.

She didn't need other people. She was a strong, independent woman, damn it.

She didn't need a protector.

So what the hell was she doing ensconced in a strange man's house, locked in and safeguarded by a state-of-the-art security system?

A plaintive meow beside her interrupted her fretful musings. His Highness gazed up at her with baleful blue eyes, his dark face framed by a plastic Elizabethan collar the vet had provided to keep him from licking his shoulder stitches.

"I'm sorry, Hizzy. We all have our crosses to bear."

"Everything okay?"

Mike's voice behind her made her jump and sent Hizzy shooting under the desk, his collar slapping against the wood and sending him sprawling at her feet. Charlie picked up the cat and whirled the chair around to look at Mike, who shot her an apologetic look.

"Yeah, peachy," she answered drily.

"Sorry about that. I'm heading to the office—I have a meeting this afternoon. You sure you're good here by myself?"

"Of course. I'll be fine."

"Help yourself to anything in the fridge. Don't worry about answering the phone—the answering service will get it. If I need to reach you, I'll call your cell phone."

"Yes, Mom."

He grinned. "I'll be back soon. I can grab something on my way home for dinner if you like. There's a nice pizza place near the office—you like pepperoni?"

"Doesn't everyone?"

"I'll call if my plans change. Lock up behind me. And set the perimeter alarm."

She set the cat on the floor and followed him to the living room. "I'll be fine, Mike. This place is a fortress."

"Okay. Call if you need anything."

"Go." She nodded toward the door. After he left,

she dutifully locked the door behind her and checked the security system box to make sure the perimeter alarms were set.

Then she returned to the cozy office, where Hizzy sat impatiently in the desk chair, gazing at her through slightly crossed eyes.

"If I take off the collar, do you swear you won't chew your stitches?"

He uttered a mournful meow.

With a sigh, she pulled the edges of the collar apart, releasing him from the plastic cone. He immediately started licking his shoulder.

"If you chew those stitches, the cone goes back on," she warned and set him on the floor by the chair.

She'd gotten behind on some of her work projects while she was dealing with the problems with her car and the vandalism of her house, so she buckled down to handling those tasks, checking every few minutes to make sure Hizzy hadn't started picking at his stitches.

An hour later, she had worked her way through the three most time-sensitive documents on her to-do list and was about to tackle the fourth when a loud trilling noise sent a shudder of surprise skating down her back.

The phone trilled a second time. It sat in a base on the right side of the desk, next to the crook-necked lamp. The phone display lit up with a phone number and a name.

Craig Bearden for Senate.

Charlie stared at the number, first with confusion,

then with a flood of dismay. Why was Craig Bearden's campaign office calling Mike Strong?

Maybe it's a campaign call, Charlie. Stop being so suspicious.

Only one way to be sure. She picked up the phone. "Hello?"

"Is Mike Strong available?" The voice on the other line sounded vaguely familiar. It wasn't Craig Bearden, however. Bearden's voice was a rich, sonorous baritone. The tenor voice on the line spoke in clipped tones, with only a hint of a Kentucky accent.

"Mr. Strong isn't in. May I take a message?"

"This is Randall Feeney. I'd like to reschedule our appointment and apologize for missing our meeting two days ago."

Charlie's stomach sank. Now she knew why the voice sounded familiar. Randall Feeney had been Craig Bearden's chief aide since his early days on the county commission, back when Alice had still been alive.

She cleared her throat. "I'm sorry. I don't know his schedule. May I have him call you back?"

There was a brief pause on the other end of the line. "I'll call him back later," Feeney said. He hung up without saying goodbye.

Charlie set the phone back on the base and slumped in her chair, her mind racing. So, Mike had made an appointment with Randall Feeney, just a couple of days after Charlie showed up in his self-defense class.

Was that a coincidence?

She didn't think so.

She opened her purse and pulled her phone from the inside pocket, pulling up her list of contacts. She'd had five different phones since Alice's death, but she had always put Alice's number in her contact list on the new phone, as if that one small gesture would keep Alice alive for her somehow.

Had the Beardens changed their number? Would someone answer if she pressed Send?

Her finger trembled over the phone screen for a long moment. Then she set the phone on the desk in front of her, releasing a long, shaky breath.

She wasn't ready to deal with the Beardens yet. So if she wanted to know why Mike Strong had contacted Craig Bearden's campaign office, she'd just have to ask him herself.

She picked up her phone, shoved it in her pocket and grabbed the jacket hanging on the back of the chair.

And she had to do it as soon as possible, before she lost her nerve.

Chapter Eight

Rebecca Cameron was a formidable woman. Not just because she was sleekly beautiful and graceful, a woman of impeccable manners and dazzling intellect. But she was a woman who'd come from humble beginnings, an African American girl raised by a steel worker and a kindergarten teacher in the deepest South, who'd risen above discrimination and oppression with dignity and determination to become one of the most well-respected diplomats in the Foreign Service.

With her steely will, she had faced down the most aggressively domineering men in the halls of power and won her battles with a smile. And it was with that same core of iron she greeted Mike with a cool smile and waved him into the seat in front of her desk.

"So," she said with no preamble, "why have you contacted the Craig Bearden campaign office?"

Mike tried not to fidget like a kid in the principal's office. "I was doing a background check."

The arch of Cameron's perfect eyebrows rose a

notch. "I wasn't aware your job description included investigations."

"Technically, it doesn't," Mike admitted, holding her gaze with a little steely determination of his own. "But one of my self-defense students pinged my radar—"

"And you thought you'd look into his background?"

"Her," he corrected. "And I discussed it with Maddox Heller first."

"Ah." She sat back, relaxing a little. Her long fingers steepled over her flat stomach as she held his gaze thoughtfully. She was a musician, he remembered. A violinist. Those long fingers had plucked strings in concert halls across the globe.

Her continuing silence started to make him nervous again. "Is that why you wanted to see me?"

"Not entirely. But the other matter can wait for now. I'm rather more interested in your impromptu investigation. Why did you contact Mr. Bearden?"

"If I may ask, how did you learn that I did?"

"Mr. Bearden, his wife and I have mutual friends. We've met several times in the past, and when one of my employees made contact with his campaign, he wanted to know why."

"I see. What did you tell him?"

She smiled. "I told him you were doing a background check on someone looking for work with one of our clients."

"And did that appease him?"

"He wanted to know who we were vetting."

"And you didn't know."

Cameron's expression made clear how little she enjoyed being asked a question she couldn't answer. "I told him you were working under a different division and I would contact you directly for the information." She sat forward again, closing the distance between them until he felt the intensity of her focus. "Which I am now doing."

"Her name is Charlotte Winters. I asked Maddox Heller to do a preliminary background check on her—confirm her name, address, that sort of thing. He discovered she was a person of interest in a murder."

Cameron's eyes narrowed. "Whose?"

Mike could tell from her tone that she already suspected the truth. "Alice Bearden's."

"I see." Cameron released a slow breath. "Is she still?"

"If she is, she's never been charged."

"What do you think of her?"

The memory of Charlie's quirky smile flitted through his mind, along with her fresh soap-and-water scent. He pictured her long limbs, her coltish gait, her husky drawl and her raspy laugh, and he tried to imagine her hitting Alice Bearden with a car and driving away without trying to help her.

"I don't think she could have done it," he said aloud before he could stop himself.

"But you're still looking into her past?"

"There have been a couple of new developments." He told Cameron about the car tampering and the break-in at Charlie's house. "Her cat was injured in the vandalism attack. If Charlie had been home, she might have been the one who was hurt."

"And this has something to do with Alice Bearden's death?" Cameron's voice was tight with doubt.

"I don't know," he admitted. "It seems unlikely that something that happened so long ago would suddenly put her life in danger now. Nothing's changed in the case, as far as I've been able to tell." Although, he hadn't contacted the police to see if there might have been a new development, had he? There was a Mercerville cop in his intermediate self-defense course, Archer Trask.

The same cop he'd seen locked up in a tense conversation with Charlie just yesterday.

"What are you thinking?" Cameron asked.

"I'm thinking I need to ask a few more questions. Which is why I tried to talk to Craig Bearden or at least someone who works for him."

"I told Craig he should speak to you. I'm sure you'll be hearing from him or someone in his campaign soon."

"Good."

"What about the woman—Ms. Winters? Does she have a safe place to stay until her home has been better secured?"

To his mortification, Mike felt heat rise up his neck. Was he blushing? He hadn't blushed since third grade. But he knew better than to lie to one of his bosses. All three of them—Cameron, Heller and the third partner, Alexander Quinn—had a long history of uncovering secrets people wanted to keep hidden.

"She's staying at my place," he said.

Cameron's gaze was expressionless and she said nothing, letting his last words ring in the silence between them.

"I have a spare room and a good security system. I'm close enough to reach her quickly if she needs my help."

"That's rather…altruistic of you."

"I can also keep an eye on her," he added, trying not to sound defensive. "If she's done something to invite danger into her life, I'll be in a good position to figure out what it is."

"Makes sense," Cameron said in a tone that suggested it did no such thing. "Perhaps, given your proximity now, you should ask her a few questions about herself. Get the information straight from the source."

Well. Didn't he feel stupid now. "You're right. I should."

Cameron pushed her chair back and stood. "I may ask you for your help with a project in a week or two, but for now, I think you should follow your instincts about Charlie Winters. If she is using our academy for questionable reasons, we need to know so that we can put a stop to it. And if she's genuinely in trouble, well, putting a stop to trouble is one of our prime directives, isn't it?"

Mike stood as well, aware he was being dismissed. "I'll keep Heller informed of what I find out."

"Do that." Cameron walked him to the door. "And do take care."

He left her office and took a left toward the gymnasium. While he was here, he might as well put a little time in with the weights. He hadn't had a chance to work out since Charlie Winters had crashed his life, and working out helped him clear the clutter from his mind and think.

He had a lot to think about.

But he didn't make it to the weight room. A door opened down the hall, a door from outside, letting in a gust of wind and rain. A tall, long-limbed silhouette filled the rectangle of light before the door closed behind it, plunging the end of the corridor into darkness again.

The dark figure moved toward him, into the dim light shed by the recessed lights in the ceiling. It was Charlie, drenched from head to foot, her red hair dark and curling, and her sweater and jeans plastered to her body, revealing unexpected curves that her loose-fitting clothing usually concealed.

"What the hell are you doing here?" he blurted, taking in her bedraggled appearance. "Did you walk here in the rain?"

Her hazel eyes were wide and dark in her pale face, and she was shivering. "You had a phone call. I took a message."

Even through chattering teeth, she conveyed an unmistakable tone of anger. He took an instinctive step back from her, out of her reach.

"Yeah? It was important enough to risk your life and health to walk a mile in a cold rain to get here? Wouldn't a phone call have been more logical?"

Her eyes flashed irritation at him. "Are you mocking me?"

He shook his head quickly. "I'm just trying to understand why you're here."

"I'm here," she said tightly, her teeth still clacking together as she spoke, "because the person who called was a man named Randall Feeney."

Oh. "You answered my phone?"

"Is that a problem?"

"You could have let the voice mail pick up." He tried to sound nonchalant, but he didn't seem to be succeeding, if the thunderclouds in her expression were anything to go by.

"I might have, but the name was familiar. And insatiable curiosity is one of my worst flaws." Her hair was dripping rainwater down her face in rivulets; she pushed the soaked curls back away from her face and ran her palms over her damp cheeks. "Why did you want a meeting with Randall Feeney?"

"Listen, I'll be glad to talk to you about this. But you're dripping all over the hall. You have to be freezing." He put his hand on her arm, felt the icy chill of her wet sweater and shivered himself. "Let's get you into some dry clothes, how about it? Before you become hypothermic."

She pulled her arm away from his grasp. "Don't handle me, okay? Just tell me the truth. Are you investigating me or something?"

"Why would you think that?"

"Because you've taken an unusual interest in my well-being all of a sudden. Coming to my rescue, standing guard over me and now moving me into your house, where you can keep an eye on me. Am I a suspect?"

"I don't know," he admitted. "I just know that you didn't join my self-defense course out of the blue, for no reason. You had an agenda. You pinged my danger radar the very first day."

"Is that why you put me in your intermediate course?"

"No, I told you the truth about why I switched you to the new class. But I can't help but wonder at the coincidence of your starting a self-defense class just a couple of days before your car's brakes were tampered with and your house was trashed by an intruder."

She stared back at him wordlessly for a moment. Then her gaze dropped, and she lifted shaky hands to her head again, shoving her fingers through her damp hair. "I'm freezing."

"I know. Let's find you something to change into."

THE SWEATSHIRT AND jersey-knit workout pants borrowed from one of Mike's female colleagues were a little short for Charlie's long limbs, but they were dry and blessedly warm. She huddled in a shivering knot in the chair in front of Mike's desk and watched him dig through a battered military-green footlocker until he found what he was looking for—an olive drab blanket that looked as if it had seen a few rough tours of duty.

"Sit forward," he said gruffly. She did as he said,

and he wrapped the blanket around her shoulders. "It's warmer than it looks."

She pulled the blanket more closely around her as he took his seat behind the desk. "Thanks."

"Warmer?"

She nodded.

"Ready to tell me why you walked all the way here in the rain?"

"I told you."

"You found out I was trying to make a meeting with someone from Craig Bearden's campaign." His eyes narrowed. "But you didn't explain why that was alarming enough to make you come dashing over here in the middle of a storm."

"Why did you contact Randall Feeney?"

He didn't answer immediately. Instead, he leaned back in his chair and looked at her with an uncomfortably direct gaze, as if taking her measure. The silence unspooling between them had become uncomfortable before he finally spoke. "You set off my radar in class."

"I know. You told me that."

"I asked one of my associates here to look into your background."

She stared at him. "You did a background check on me?"

"I needed to know if you had an ulterior motive for joining my class. What we do here at Campbell Cove Academy is important work. We're training people to protect themselves, their families and their communities in the case of a terrorist attack or some other mass-casualty event. Or to prevent those events, if possible."

"I know your company's mission statement." She waved one hand with impatience. "You actually saw me as a potential threat?"

"I have to assume everyone is a potential threat," he answered with equal exasperation. "I have to run all the scenarios in my head and make sure I'm not letting an enemy through the gates."

"Which you thought I was."

"I thought you might be, so I had someone check your background."

"And that led you to Craig Bearden." She wiped a drop of rainwater away from her forehead, wishing she'd asked for a towel to dry her hair.

"You were with Alice Bearden the night she was killed. The police considered you a person of interest for a long time."

"I wasn't driving the car that hit Alice."

"So what happened that night?"

She looked at him through narrowed eyes. "Didn't your background check give you all the details?"

"Not everything. Not the things you could tell me."

She tucked her knees up to her chest and pulled her cold, bare toes beneath the soft cotton of the olive drab blanket. "Why does it matter now? It was so long ago."

"Ten years, right?"

She nodded. "Give or take a few months."

He rose and came around the desk to stand in front

of her. "Did it have anything to do with your decision to take a self-defense course?"

How could she answer his question without revealing just how much of a hidden agenda she really had? She hadn't told anyone in her life about her decision to take a new look at Alice's death because everybody, including Alice's parents, considered her death a closed chapter. She'd died in a hit-and-run accident. Period. Someone had gotten away with vehicular homicide, but it wasn't as if her death had been premeditated, was it?

Except Charlie was starting to think maybe it had been premeditated. Or, at the very least, her death wasn't nearly as cut-and-dried as the police reports had finally concluded.

Charlie's memories were incomplete. But fragments had begun to emerge in her dreams recently, revealing enough mysteries and unanswered questions to pique her lifelong curiosity.

Charlie needed the questions answered. The mysteries solved.

But could Mike Strong understand that need? And if he did, would he really be willing to help her find those answers?

"Just say it, Charlie." He crouched in front of her chair, his voice low and soft, a seduction. Not just a physical temptation, though she was already resigned to her physical attraction to him. It was the emotional attraction she felt, the all-too-enticing desire to pile all her fears and troubles on his extrawide shoulders and let him handle things for a while, that left her feeling upended and unsettled.

She told herself she couldn't let herself surrender. She'd survived the harsh world of her childhood by never depending on anyone else for anything.

Could she really start now?

But she hadn't exactly done a great job of going it alone, had she?

He touched her hand where it clutched the blanket. "You want to tell me, but you're afraid."

She met his gaze, remaining silent.

"Do you remember something new?" When she didn't answer, he added, "Someone seems to think you do."

He was right. And she was foolish to think this time she could handle things alone. She had to trust someone.

Maybe it could be Mike.

"Tell me, Charlie." His growly whisper sent a shiver through her. "Someone tried to kill you. They trashed your house. They're not playing games. They're serious."

"I know." If she let herself think about it, the memory of pressing her foot on the brake pedal and feeling no response at all could send panic rocketing through her again. "I just don't know why."

"Are you sure?"

"Mike, I don't remember most of the night Alice died."

"Why? Were you drunk?"

"I shouldn't have been. I've never been much of

a drinker. I grew up with drinkers, and all alcohol ever did for them was raise their levels of stupidity to legendary heights." She shook her head. "I wouldn't have drunk enough to pass out. I just wouldn't have."

"So why don't you remember?"

He was too close, the heat of his body too intense. She pushed back her chair and rose, wrapping the blanket tightly around her as she crossed to the window. Outside, the day was drenched and gloomy, drizzle pebbling the window to render the view of the parking lot misty and dreamlike.

"I think maybe I was drugged."

She'd never said the words out loud before, never let herself consider the ramifications. But it was the one thing that made sense of what little she could remember of that night.

"Were you—" Mike's voice was unexpectedly close behind her.

"No," she said quickly, turning to face him. In a bar situation, a dose of Rohypnol or GHB—gamma hydroxybutyric acid—was usually the precursor of sexual assault. Charlie hadn't felt as if she'd been assaulted in any way when she woke cold and damp in her backyard early the next morning after her night out with Alice.

Well, her head had been fuzzy and throbbing, and her memory was a wide vista of nothingness, but her clothes were all in place and she didn't have any of the morning-after sensations she associated with sex. "I don't think I was raped. I think I was…removed from the situation."

He cocked his head. "Meaning?"

"I think Alice went to the Headhunter in hopes of running into someone else. She took me along so she didn't spend the whole night fending off pickup artists."

"Did you tell the cops your theory?"

"I wasn't sure. By the time I had a chance to think anything through, the story was already set in the news. Bar sells alcohol to underage teens. One of them dies in a hit-and-run accident outside the bar. The grieving father vows to honor his daughter's memory by working to close the gaps in the law that allow those things to happen." She shook her head. "Nobody wanted to hear an alternative theory."

"I do," Mike said gently.

"So do I," she said. "But the problem is, I still don't have one. At least, not one I can prove."

Mike lifted his hands to her cheeks, his palms warm against her cold cheeks. His thumbs brushed lightly across her cheeks, smearing moisture, and she realized she had been crying.

"Then let's find some proof," he said.

"How? It was ten years ago."

"We do what a cop would do," he said with a gruff firmness that gave her an idea what he must have been like as a Marine. "Tomorrow night, we'll start at the scene of the crime."

Chapter Nine

Charlie hadn't expected to sleep much on her first night at Mike's place. Besides the strange bed and the strange man in the room across the hall, she'd also had to contend with a grumpy Siamese cat in a plastic cone collar and a scaredy-cat tortoiseshell cat who jumped at every strange noise.

But the walk in the rain and the stress of the afternoon as she and Mike mapped out their plan for a trip to the Headhunter Bar on Saturday night had apparently wrung out all of the adrenaline left in her body, and she slept all night, waking only when Hizzy plopped onto her chest and butted her with the sharp edge of his plastic cone.

"Ow!" she complained, pushing him gently away. "You're a menace with that thing."

There was a knock on the door and Mike's muffled voice from the other side. "Are you up?"

"Getting there," she called, rolling to a sitting position on the edge of the bed. "Give me a few minutes."

"Breakfast is almost ready."

Breakfast, she discovered when she finished dressing and headed into the kitchen, was again scrambled eggs and toast, plus hot coffee that hit the spot. While they were eating, Hizzy wandered into the kitchen, bumping his cone against the door frame on the way to her side.

"How much longer does he have to wear the cone of shame?" Mike asked.

"The vet said I could take it off for a few hours at a time as long as I could keep an eye on him and make sure he doesn't chew his stitches." She bent and offered Hizzy a bite of eggs. "This reminds me, I need to go back home and get the extra bag of cat food I left in the mudroom. This morning I used up the last of the food I brought with me."

"I'll swing by and get it for you," Mike offered. "I've got to head that way to meet with Randall Feeney."

Charlie stopped with her coffee cup halfway to her mouth. "He got back to you?"

"I called him back. While you were in the shower yesterday afternoon." Mike bent and held out a piece of egg for Hizzy. The cat sniffed at it and finally nibbled the food from Mike's fingers.

"And you didn't tell me?"

"You were tired and stressed. I thought it could wait for this morning."

"What are you going to say to him?"

Mike wiped his hands on a paper towel. "That I was doing a background check on you."

"What if he asks you why?"

"I'll tell him it's routine for anyone who attends any of our classes."

Charlie shook her head. "Don't tell him I'm taking classes at the academy."

"Why not?"

"I just don't want him to know," she said, not certain why she felt that way.

Mike gave her a curious look, but he just nodded. "I'll say it's for a potential employer, then."

"That's good."

"Speaking of employers, did everything go okay yesterday? Your computer setup working like it's supposed to?"

"Everything was fine. I managed to get all caught up, so I won't need to do any mop-up over the weekend."

"Great, because we have plans this evening."

The thought of their excursion into Mercerville's seedy side made Charlie's breakfast settle in a queasy lump at the pit of her stomach. "Right."

He reached across the table. "If you don't want to do this, say so. I'll figure out something else."

The temptation to back out of their plan was unexpectedly potent. But she'd never be able to look herself in the mirror if she chickened out. "No. We're going. I need to see if I can remember anything else."

He gave her an odd look. "Anything else? Have you remembered something already?"

She hadn't told him about the dreams. She wasn't all that sure she thought they were real memories herself. Dreams could be deceiving.

But her behavior would suggest she'd already made up her mind. If she didn't believe those dream-memories had meaning, she wouldn't be dredging up the most horrific night of her life, would she?

"Charlie?"

"I've been having dreams," she said.

STILL PONDERING THE things Charlie had told him, Mike pulled his truck into the driveway of Charlie's house and sat there for a moment, the engine idling, while he took a look around the neighborhood from the safety of the cab. Yesterday's rain had given way to watery sunshine brightening inch by inch as morning crept toward midday.

Despite the improved weather, the other houses in the neighborhood were still and silent. No children played in the winter-brown yards. No home owners raked away the last of the autumn leaves.

People must keep to themselves in this area, Mike thought. He'd talked to the Campbell Cove police officer who'd come to Charlie's house the day the intruder trashed the place. Officer Bentley had canvassed the neighborhood to see if anyone had spotted the intruders. No one had seen anything, although the nearest neighbor had arrived home early from work the day of the vandalism. Bentley had theorized that the sound of the neighbor coming home at an unexpected time might have sent the vandals running before they finished the job.

What Bentley hadn't said was how the vandals would have known what time the neighbors usually came home in the first place. It suggested a level of surveillance that didn't seem likely for a random intruder.

Someone was afraid of what Charlie was starting to remember. That was the only possible reason for the things happening to her now.

Charlie told him that she'd tried contacting Craig Bearden a few weeks ago, after the dreams started. She'd left a message, telling him she wanted to talk to him about Alice's death. She'd even mentioned the memories she was starting to recover, hoping he'd be interested enough to call her back and help her figure out what had really happened that night.

Could someone at the campaign office have intercepted the message? Or had Craig received it himself and mentioned it to the wrong person?

For that matter, could Craig Bearden himself have been involved in what had happened to his daughter?

Pondering the possibilities, Mike walked up the path to Charlie's porch. The key Charlie had given him opened the front door. He made a mental note to call a locksmith to change the front dead bolt, though he wasn't sure it would make a difference. Whoever had wrecked Charlie's house a couple of days ago had gotten in without forcing the lock. Either they'd had access to Charlie's keys or they knew how to beat a lock.

He'd talk her into spending the money on a decent alarm system, too. Campbell Cove Security Services worked with a good outfit who would do the work for her at a reasonable price.

The living room looked depressingly bare, now that

he and Charlie had moved the worst of the destruction to the alley behind her house. He could pack most of the bigger pieces into the bed of his truck and carry them to the dump outside town, he thought. Then maybe the trash collection truck could take the rest.

The desolation made the house seem colder than it should have been on that mild December day. It was lifeless without its vibrant inhabitant and her two cat companions.

He paused halfway down the hall, drawn toward the bedroom and the quilt-covered bed where he and Charlie had sat two nights before, talking about themselves in hushed tones in the dark.

He ran his hands over the intricate pattern of the bedcover, noting the hand stitching and the faded patches that suggested the quilt had been handmade years ago. A family heirloom? A thrift store treasure?

There was so much he didn't know about her, and normally such a thought didn't bother him. He was a results-oriented sort of guy. Get in, get the job done, get out. He didn't bother too much about personalities and avoided thinking about emotions and motivations, except to make sure they didn't come between him and his goal.

But Charlie made him want to know more. Sometimes, meeting her gaze, he sensed there was a whole other world beneath the reflective mountain-pool eyes, a place of mysteries and wonders he wanted to investigate. How much was she still keeping secret from him? What was she hiding, and why?

He tugged the quilt from the bed and folded it into

a neat square. It would fit nicely on his spare bed, he thought, and it would make her feel a little more at home. Maybe help her relax her guard and share a few of her secrets with him.

He set the blanket on the kitchen table and took a step into the mudroom.

There was a flash of movement. He had the impression of something black and red moving toward him in a rush, then pain exploded in the side of his head, sending him reeling hard into the door frame. Agony bloomed like a noxious cloud, filling his stunned brain with a blinding mist the color of dried blood. For a moment, he could hear nothing, feel nothing but throbbing pain filling his head. Then sensations returned in a flash of light and noise. Sunlight pierced the mudroom window and into his brain like a dagger. He heard a door open and slam shut behind him, the sound like a hammer blow.

He pushed himself away from the wall, wincing at the thudding ache that had replaced the fuzzy sensation in his brain. Staggering to the back door to look through the four-paned window, he scanned the backyard. Behind her house, the woods encroached on the lawn, casting a shadowy gloom over the vista. At first, he saw nothing but the faint sway of the winter-bare tree limbs rattled by the light breeze. But movement caught his eye, and he spotted a man dressed in dark green camouflage zigzagging through the underbrush several yards from the house.

He opened the door and headed toward the fleeing figure, but his feet didn't want to cooperate with each other. He tripped over the uneven ground, staggering sideways. He caught himself before he fell to the ground, but by the time he regained his balance, he could no longer see the man in camouflage. He watched the woods for several moments, trying to reacquire his target, but he quickly realized the effort was futile. The intruder had gotten too large a head start, and Mike's brain was too fuzzy from the knock on the head for him to make up any ground, even if he'd managed to catch sight of the fleeing man.

He lifted his hand to the side of his head and felt the sticky heat of blood oozing from a tender spot on the side of his forehead. He reentered the house and looked around the mudroom, wondering what had hit him. There was a dented can of stewed tomatoes lying on the floor beside an otherwise neat row of canned goods on a set of shelves against the inner wall of the mudroom. Up on the top shelf, packed inside a large plastic bin with a lid, there was a large unopened bag of cat food.

He reached up to bring down the bin, grimacing at the pain shooting through his head. He thought better of taking the bag of food out of the plastic bin—if Charlie had stored it there, she must have had a good reason why—and just carried the bin into the kitchen and set it on the table next to the quilt.

Then he grabbed a few paper towels and carried them with him into the bathroom to take a look at the damage the intruder had done.

The cut on the side of his head was evenly curved, confirming his suspicious that he'd been coldcocked with the can of tomatoes. Fortunately, the can had caught him on the side of his forehead, where the thicker bone had protected his brain from the blow. A few inches lower, the thin bone of his temples might not have sustained the hit nearly as well.

There was a surprising amount of blood for so small and shallow a wound, but head wounds tended to bleed a lot. Mike had sustained worse injuries in his time in the Marine Corps. He mopped up the mess and pressed against the tender spot to stop the bleeding, then took a closer look.

The skin was already turning blue around the wound, and it would probably only get worse as the day went on, but the split in the skin wasn't deep enough to require stitches at least. He found a couple of adhesive bandage strips in the medicine cabinet and covered the cut. With the wound hidden from view by the bandages, he almost looked back to normal.

Well, except for the blood staining the left side of his shirt. But his jacket should cover the stains for the drive home.

But he wasn't quite ready to leave yet. Someone had come back to Charlie's house looking for something.

What had he been looking for?

"WHAT DO YOU THINK, Nellie? Should we take off the cone of shame and see if Hizzy can behave?" Charlie scratched behind Nellie's brindle-colored ears and looked at His Highness sitting in front of her, blue eyes staring back at her with haughty disdain.

He had finally stopped bumping into everything with the small plastic cone fastened around his head, but he was clearly unhappy with its continuing presence.

The wound on his shoulder wouldn't be easy for him to reach, even if he twisted his head as far as it would turn, she decided. "Come here, Hizzy. Let's get that thing off you."

The cat eyed her warily for a moment before he slowly slinked across the floor to her and let her pet his head. She unfastened the plastic cone collar and eased it from his neck. Immediately, he started to groom himself.

She watched to make sure he didn't start chewing his stitches, but he seemed more interested in washing his paws and his face.

The trill of her cell phone ringing made her nerves jangle and sent both of the cats skittering away to stare at her from opposite corners of the room. She pulled the phone from the pocket of her jeans. Mike's number. "Hello?"

"Everything going okay there?" He sounded a little strange, she thought, his voice a little thick.

"Everything's fine. Did you find the cat food okay?"

"Yeah. You want me to bring the box it's in, too?"

"If you don't want the cats to rip into the cat food bag and leave food scattered all over your house, yes."

"Ah. That's why it's in the box."

"I thought you had cats before."

"It's been a while. Since I was a kid. I didn't bother with where to store the cat food back then."

"You sound strange. Everything okay?"

"Yeah."

She didn't find his tone convincing. "Did something happen?"

There was a long pause, then he sighed. "There was someone in the house when I got here."

"My God." She tightened her grip on the phone. "Did you see him?"

"Only at a distance. He caught me off guard and got away. I didn't get a good look."

"Caught you off guard? Are you okay?"

"I'm fine. I'll tell you all about it when I get home. But while I'm still here—do you have any idea what the intruder might have been looking for?"

"No," she said without hesitation. If she possessed anything that might prove dangerous to anyone else in the world, it was locked inside her brain, unreachable even by her.

"Then what was he here for?"

To stop her, she thought. To keep her from ever remembering what happened that night in Mercerville.

"I think maybe he was there to kill me," she said.

Suddenly, from somewhere down the hall, she heard a loud electronic beep. Over the phone, Mike uttered a soft profanity.

"What is that?" she asked, pushing to her feet to follow the sound.

As she reached the source and saw the electronic monitor with one light blinking bright red in time with the beeping noise, Mike said, his voice tight with dismay, "It's the perimeter alarm. Someone's moving around outside the house."

The nerves the beeping noise had set jangling were rattling hard now, making her shake as she tightened her grasp on the phone before it fell from her trembling fingers. "What should I do? Will the system notify the cops?"

"No. It can be set off by an animal crossing the sensor beam. I don't have it set for automatic notification."

"Should I call the cops?"

"I'm a lot closer. I'll be there before your call gets forwarded to the right people. Just hang tight. I'm heading out now." Over the phone, she heard a symphony of disparate sounds—Mike's rapid breathing, a few strange, rattling thuds and then a door slamming shut. A few thumps and bangs later, she heard the sound of the truck engine roaring to life. "Stay on the phone with me, Charlie. Whatever you do, don't put down the phone."

He was scaring her now. "Shouldn't I go see who's at the door?"

"No," he said quickly, "don't go near the door."

"I could look through the security lens—"

"The door may be steel reinforced, but the windows aren't bullet resistant. You could be targeted. Stay away from doors and windows. Where are you now?"

"In the hall by the alarm keypad."

"Stay right there. I'll be home in minutes."

She heard three hard rapping noises coming from down the hall. "I think someone is knocking on the door."

"Don't answer it, Charlie."

"Not moving," she assured him.

Two more knocks rattled the door. "What if it's someone looking for you?"

"They'll just have to try back later," he answered. "Charlie, I know you're as curious as a kitten—"

"I'm not stupid," she snapped back. "Trust me. I'm not moving from this hall until you get here."

"Good." Mike fell silent, apparently concentrating on driving. From the sound of the truck's engine, he was driving way too fast for the narrow mountain roads between her house and his, but she had a feeling he was a good enough driver to handle it.

In fact, she was certain he was one hell of a man to have in her corner no matter what the situation. She took comfort from the knowledge that he was on the way and would be here soon. It was almost enough to calm her jangling nerves.

Until she heard the scrape of metal on metal coming from the front of the house.

Chapter Ten

There was a soft gasp on Charlie's end of the phone, and then all Mike could hear was rapid breathing.

"Charlie?" He tapped the Bluetooth earpiece. "Are you still there?"

"Someone's coming in the door!" Her voice was a panicky hiss of breath. "Oh, my God—"

"Go to my bedroom and lock the door behind you. There's a table by the bed—drag it in front of the door. Then go to my closet and get inside."

"Okay." He heard the soft thud of her footsteps as she hurried down the hallway and into his bedroom, then the scrape of the bedside table moving. A moment later, she spoke again. "I'm in the closet. There's no way to lock the door."

"I know. I just wanted you in the closet because that's where I keep my weapons."

There was a brief pause, then she whispered, "Oh."

"Do you know anything about handguns or rifles?"

"I've shot guns before," she said softly. "But it was a long time ago."

"I don't think they've changed that much since then. Can you see anything in the closet?"

"No," she whispered.

"There's a light switch just inside the door."

He heard a muted click and a huff of breath from Charlie. "That's better."

"See the gun safe now?"

"The big safe with a keypad?"

"That's the one." He gave her the number combination and waited for her to punch it in.

"It's not working," she said, her voice rising with alarm.

He knew the sound of panic when he heard it. "Stop, Charlie. Stop a second and just take a couple of deep breaths, okay? In and out." He breathed with her, even though his own body was so pumped with adrenaline, he felt as if ants were crawling all over him. "In and out."

He was only a couple of blocks away. Another block and he'd have his own preparations to worry about. His Glock 19 was loaded and snug in a hip holster, so he could go in hot. But he still needed to be prepared mentally as well as tactically, especially with a civilian in danger.

"Try it again," he said, pulling to a quick stop at the corner stop sign. He could almost see his house from here. Just a few more yards...

"It's open," she breathed. Then she sucked in a swift breath. "Good grief, how many people do you plan to shoot?"

His lips curved, trying to picture his gun cabinet

from her point of view. He owned several pistols, a shotgun and a rifle with a sniper scope. He'd hoped he'd never have to use any of them, but life in a free country came with costs.

"Do any of them look familiar?"

She was quiet a second. "My brother had a Mossberg shotgun. I know how to load it, and from there, it's pretty much point and shoot."

"Okay. Load it. But don't shoot it unless your life is absolutely in danger, understand? I don't want to get shot when I get there."

"I'll sit right here and try not to shoot anyone," she muttered.

"I'm nearly there." He could see his house now. There was a dark blue sedan parked in the driveway. He didn't recognize it. He didn't see anyone in the vehicle or standing on his porch, so apparently the driver had somehow made it past his dead bolt and entered the house.

He drove past, parked on the street two houses down and used the neighbors' yards and houses to provide cover as he headed for the back of his house. He could still hear Charlie's soft, rapid breathing in the Bluetooth earpiece. "I'm on my way, Charlie. Can you hear anything outside the closet?"

"I think maybe footsteps. I'm not sure."

"Nobody's tried to get in the bedroom?"

"No."

"Great. Hang tight. I'm hanging up now so I can concentrate, okay?"

"Okay." She didn't sound as if she meant it.

"It's almost over. I promise. The next thing you'll hear is me coming in the back door."

"You gonna bust in, SWAT-style?" she asked.

"You like the sound of that, do you?" He kept his voice light.

"Sounds kind of sexy," she admitted, her own voice a little less shaky. "Once things are under control, I won't complain if you take off your shirt and smolder at me a little bit."

He couldn't hold back a grin. "You read too many books, Charlie."

"One can never read too many books." She sounded considerably calmer now. Clearly, a little flirtation was Charlie's version of relaxation.

"Talk to you soon." He disconnected the call, pulled off the Bluetooth headset and shoved it in his pocket.

He was at the back door now. He stuck the key in the lock, taking care to turn it as quietly as possible, glad that he'd oiled the door hinges recently. The back door swung open with little noise, and he stepped into the kitchen and swept the room with his pistol.

Clear.

He heard a soft scraping noise coming from the front room. A chair leg moving across the floor?

Silently, he crept up the hall, leading with the Glock. He paused just clear of the doorway into the living room and listened. He heard breathing now. Quiet. Calm. If the intruder was nervous about breaking into Mike's house, he showed no outward sign of it.

Edging forward, Mike peeked around the door frame and caught sight of the intruder. Tall, raw-boned, with wavy blond hair cut short, poking at the wood in the fireplace, trying to coax the flickering flames to life.

He dropped the pistol to his side. "Mom?"

Amelia Strong gave a start, whirling to face him, the fire poker she held brandished like a weapon. "Michael, you scared the stuffing out of me!"

He stared at her in confusion, his adrenaline rush subsiding. "What are you doing here?"

She flashed him a sheepish grin and threw her arms out to the sides. "Surprise!"

He frowned. "Surprise?"

She put the fire poker back in the stand beside the anemic fire in his hearth. "Your birthday tomorrow? You didn't call to make plans for celebrating…"

"So you decided to drive up here and take it into your own hands." He put his pistol in the holster and gave her a swift hug. "I'm sorry. I should have called and told you things had gotten crazy busy around here."

She was staring at his head. "What did you do to yourself?"

He lifted his fingers to the bandages. "It's nothing."

"My God, is that blood on your face?"

"Mom, I promise you I'm fine."

"You've been bleeding. And now that I look at you, you're looking a little sweaty and pale."

"Maybe because I thought there was a burglar in

my house," he grumbled. "When I gave you that key, it was supposed to be for emergencies only. Remember?"

"A forgotten birthday is an emergency."

"Mom, hold on a second, okay?" He put his hand up to keep her where she was, then hurried down the hallway to his bedroom. He knocked on the door. "Charlie, it's Mike. Everything's fine. You can unlock the door for me now. And leave the shotgun in the closet."

He heard the closet door open and footsteps from the other side of the door. The bedside table scraped out of the way and Charlie opened the door, looking up at him with wide eyes.

Then she launched herself at him, her long arms wrapping around his neck as she buried her face in his neck.

"Whoa, there." He enfolded her in his embrace, breathing deeply of the clean smell he now associated with her alone. "Everything's okay. It was just a false alarm."

She pulled her head back. "You mean nobody was here? I swear I heard someone coming in. And just a minute ago, I thought I heard voices."

"Michael?" His mother's voice sounded uncertain.

Mike and Charlie both turned to look at her.

"I'm sorry. Did I interrupt something?" Amelia asked.

Mike took a deep breath and turned to look at Charlie. "Charlie, meet your intruder. My mom."

"So, of course, since I hadn't heard from him in over a week, I thought he was probably too busy to come visit me for his birthday, so I asked Lauren to watch the shop for me a few days while I went to visit my handsome son." Amelia Strong flashed Charlie a smile that had "I want grandchildren and I want them now" written all over it. "So, Michael, where have you been hiding Charlie?"

"In the closet," Charlie quipped with a nervous laugh.

"Charlie is a client," Mike said carefully. "She's dealing with an unknown stalker. She's staying here a few days so I can keep an eye on her."

"And she brought her cat?" Amelia arched one sandy eyebrow at His Highness, who had settled next to her on the sofa and was watching her with crossed blue eyes.

"Cats," Charlie corrected. "Although Nellie hasn't ventured out from under the bed that much since I got here, so it's almost like there's only one cat. Except for the two food bowls." She shut up, aware she was starting to babble, something she often did when she met strangers.

She could almost see Amelia Strong striking Charlie's name from her list of potential grandchild producers with a big red marker.

She shot Mike a helpless look, her gaze snagging once again on the bandage strips stuck to the side of his head. He'd shrugged off her earlier question about it, but from her viewpoint from the armchair beside him, she caught a glimpse of drying blood on the patch of shirt she could see beneath his jacket. The fire had finally reached full blaze, driving out all the chill of the day, so she knew he had to be growing warm beneath the jacket. But he still hadn't taken it off.

What was he hiding?

"Mom, I wish you'd called ahead. I could have told you the spare room was already taken."

"Don't worry about that," she said, smiling at Charlie again. "I've already made a call to that nice bed-and-breakfast in Campbell Cove. You know, the one near your office? They said there's a room available and I can have it for three nights. So we're set, then, aren't we?"

Mike smiled at his mother, but Charlie didn't buy his cheery demeanor. Amelia didn't, either, it seemed, for her expression fell.

"I'm sorry. I should have called. I just—" She twisted her hands in frustration. "I thought I'd see more of you after you left the Marine Corps. I was counting on it."

Mike glanced at Charlie. She gave a slight nod toward his mother.

He got up and crouched in front of his mother, taking her hands. "I'm sorry. I've been so busy trying to get used to being a civilian again that I've forgotten some of the perks of not wearing a uniform anymore. I should have called you. Made plans for my birthday. And Christmas."

"You missed Thanksgiving, too," she murmured.

"But I did call."

She touched his face. "Yes, you did."

"We'll do something while you're here. Maybe drive up to Lexington and see the holiday lights?"

"Oh, and there are some lovely Christmas shops up there, too. I can pick up some new ornaments for the tree." Amelia clapped her hands. "And Charlie will come with us, right?"

"Oh, I don't think—" Charlie began.

"Absolutely," Mike said, giving her a pleading look. "Charlie's from around here, as a matter of fact. She can probably tell you all the best places to go shopping while you're in town."

"I'm not much of a shopper," she muttered.

"Don't worry about that. I'll do all the shopping." Amelia's smile was infectious. "Tomorrow, yes? I'll take my things to the B and B and rest for tonight. It's a long drive from Black Rock."

"That's a great idea, actually. Charlie and I have something we have to do tonight." Mike pushed to his feet as his mother rose, already heading for her suitcases by the door. He grabbed them for her, glancing over his shoulder at Charlie. "But I'll call you in the morning and we'll all go do something fun tomorrow. Okay?"

"It's a plan!" Amelia smiled up at him, then looked at Charlie, who had trailed along behind them because she didn't know what else to do. "It's been lovely to meet you, Charlie," she said as Mike headed out to the car with her bags. She lowered her voice. "Get that jacket off him. I think you'll find there's blood on his shirt. He's going to act as if it's no big deal, but make him let you see what he's hiding under those bandages."

The cheery good humor, Charlie realized, hid a quick and serious mind.

"Already on it," she told Amelia.

Amelia reached out and took her hand. "I like you, Charlie Winters. Mike must like you, too, to go to such lengths to protect you."

"It's his job."

"Right." Amelia squeezed Charlie's hand and headed after her son.

Mike was back in a few minutes, carrying the box with the cat food. He had also brought the quilt from her bed, she saw with surprise. "I thought you might want a little piece of home. Besides the cats, I mean."

To her surprise, tears pricked her eyes. She blinked them away. "Thank you. That was very thoughtful."

He set the box on the coffee table. "I'm sorry about all that. With my mom, I mean. She should have called first."

"Don't worry about it. A little adrenaline rush in the middle of the day gets the blood pumping." Now that the scare was over, she mostly meant it. Most of her days were spent editing technical manuals and directives for handling military demolition ordnance, which sounded a lot more exciting than it was.

"My father died not long before I left the Marines, and with my brother working in England—he's a news producer for a cable network's European bureaus—"

"Your mom just misses you?" Charlie finished for him.

"Yeah." He tugged at his jacket collar absently. "You want me to take that box into the spare room?"

"In a minute." She crossed until she stood close enough to see the first purplish hint of bruising on the side of his forehead. "But first, you want to show me that gash on your head?"

He touched the bandages with his fingertips. "Just a cut."

"Trip on something?"

He dropped his hand. "You remember that intruder in your house?"

"He did this?" She reached up and tugged the collar of his jacket aside, revealing an alarming number of bloody blotches on the front of his shirt. "Did you have a fight with him?"

"No. He hit me right off. After that, it was all catch-up. Which clearly I didn't do."

She tugged down the zipper of his jacket. "Are you hurt anywhere but your head?"

He shrugged off his jacket, his expression a valiant attempt at playing it cool. "It's just a little cut on my head. No big deal. I didn't lose consciousness or anything."

"And that's your criteria for whether or not an injury is serious?" She tugged at the edge of the lower bandage, wincing as it tugged against his wound and made him suck in a quick breath. With the first of the bandages gone, she saw a nasty, curved gash in the thin skin of his forehead. "Oh, Mike. That looks terrible. What did he hit you with?"

"A can of tomatoes, I think." Mike caught her hand as she started to lift the second bandage. "I can do it."

He pulled off the remaining bandage. The wound was about two inches long and curved like the edge of a metal can, suggesting Mike was right about what had hit him. The skin around the cuts was starting to turn an ugly shade of purple.

"Maybe you should see a doctor," she said.

"No need. I'm not concussed and the wound isn't deep enough to require stitches. I'll just give it a good wash and put something on it, mercurochrome or antibiotic ointment or something."

"Come into the kitchen. Let me get a better look at it."

His eyes narrowed. "Is this where I'm supposed to take off my shirt and smolder at you?"

"Yes." She caught his hand and tugged him with her down the hall to the kitchen. Pointing toward one of the kitchen chairs, she asked, "Where do you keep the first aid kit."

"Shh. I'm smoldering here."

"You can't smolder with your shirt on. Is the first aid kit in the bathroom?"

"In the top drawer of the sink cabinet," he said with an exaggerated sigh. "Can't we just skip right to the kissing it all better part?"

She leaned toward him, closing the distance between them until she felt his breath on her lips. Catching his stubbly chin in her fingers, she made him look at her, almost instantly regretting it. He was, quite simply, a pretty, pretty man. And all she had to do was lean forward a notch and her lips would be on his.

It took all her strength to pull her head back and say, "No."

She turned on her heel and hurried away to the bathroom, her heart pounding like a drum. She found the kit right away, but she took a moment to calm her rattled nerves.

It was just a game. A way of putting the tension of the intruder false alarm out of their minds and finding something to laugh about. That was all.

Wasn't it?

When she returned to the kitchen with the first aid kit, she found Mike at the table, tugging off his shirt to reveal the lean, toned body of an infantry Marine.

She stopped midway to the table and let out a quick breath.

"Can you tell if I have a wound back here?" he asked, his head twisted toward his back. "When I got hit by the can, I slammed into the door frame, and there's a really sore spot on this shoulder." He turned his back to her, revealing another spectacular set of muscles, along with a linear bruise from the top of his shoulder to the bottom of his rib cage.

"Just a bruise," she said, "but a pretty big one. Sure you didn't crack a rib, too?"

"No, I've had cracked ribs before. Not something you can have without knowing it." He turned back to face her. "I can treat my head wound myself."

"I can see it better," she murmured, not willing

to give up the chance to touch him, complication-free. "You think we should call the police about what happened?"

"So they could do what?"

"Take fingerprints?"

"The guy was wearing gloves." Mike's brow creased suddenly, the movement apparently pulling at the cut on his forehead, for he winced immediately afterward. "I didn't remember that until just now."

She opened the first aid kit, pulled out an antiseptic wipe packet and tore it open. "Do you remember anything else?"

"There was a scar. On the inside of his wrist. It looked kind of like a half-moon. Just below his thumb pad, I think."

"That's a lot to suddenly remember." There was no good way to get close to his injured head without stepping between his legs. But she could put aside her attraction to him long enough to nurse his injury, couldn't she? Of course she could.

He watched her approach, his green eyes smoldering as promised. He spread his legs open, daring her to come closer. "Come on, Charlie. You're the one who wanted to play nurse. Chickening out?"

She lifted her chin a notch. "Not on your life."

With a deep breath, she crossed the room and settled her hips between his thighs, forcing herself to concentrate on his oozing head wound. "Fair warning. This is probably going to hurt."

"Not if you do it right," he whispered.

Chapter Eleven

Mike cocked his head to the side to give her a better angle, slanting his gaze to hold hers. She stared back at him, her eyes shimmering like a mirror pool, hiding her thoughts. She was nothing less than a tantalizing mystery, begging to be solved.

And he wanted to be the one who uncovered all her deepest, darkest secrets, one by one.

"Come on, Charlie," he said, his voice barely above a whisper. "You can do this."

She let out a slow breath, bathing his cheek with warmth. With a gentle touch, she applied the antiseptic wipe to the open cut, wincing in sympathy at his hiss of pain. "Sorry."

"What do you think? Will I live?"

She finished cleaning the rest of the blood from the wound and took a closer look. "It's not too deep. I think you're right about not needing stitches. I guess you're probably up-to-date on your tetanus shot, since you were in the military."

"Yep," he drawled, intentionally smoldering at her again.

She cleared her throat. "Are you sure you didn't lose consciousness?"

"I saw stars, but I didn't really black out."

"Because you're remembering things you didn't remember before."

"Just that thing about the gloves. And the guy's scar."

She started to back away from him, but her feet tangled up with each other, and she started to fall backward.

Mike grabbed her, tugging her back between his legs again. He settled his hands over her hips, his thumbs drawing circles over her hip bones. "I've got you."

This was crazy. *He* was crazy.

But she felt so good beneath his hands, all interesting angles and surprising softness. She was beautiful like a mountain spring, calmly pretty on the surface but full of surprises beneath, cool currents and warm eddies, with lots of hidden dangers and delights. He wondered if she could see that beauty in herself when she looked in the mirror. He hoped she did.

She gazed back at him, her expression shifting from emotion to emotion, too fast for him to read them as they flashed across her mobile features.

So he asked. "What are you thinking?"

For a long moment, she was silent. He lifted one hand to take the hand she still had pressed against his shoulder to keep her balance, sliding his thumb over her palm.

"I was…" Her voice cracked, making him smile with satisfaction. Whatever else she was thinking, apparently she wasn't as immune to seduction as her cool exterior might suggest.

She started again. "I was wondering if there was anything else you could remember about the guy. Since you saw his wrist, could you tell if he was white or Hispanic or African American?"

"White," he said, still not letting her hand go. He held it out in front of him, his thumb slowly tracing over the angles of her knuckles. "I'd say he's probably relatively young. No older than forty or so. Or else he's in amazing shape for a man that age. He was fast getting away."

"Height? Weight?" She kept dropping her gaze to his hand, watching his fingers join his thumb in the slow exploration of her fingers.

"About as tall as I am. Maybe an inch or two shorter. A little heavier, though not much."

Her breathing had quickened, and her hazel eyes had darkened, as if reflecting storm clouds. He was getting to her. Breaking down her reserves, touching a place of pure want inside her.

The problem was, he was breaking down his own walls, the ones he'd learned to build over the years, designed to keep the rest of the world at a safe distance. A life of war had destroyed his faith in a whole lot of humanity. Even now, working at Campbell Cove Security Services, he had no illusions about his job. He wasn't a savior. He couldn't protect the innocent.

There weren't many innocents left anyway. After the things he'd seen, he was pretty sure this world was doomed to be swallowed by its own darkness, sooner or later.

He was just holding back the night as long as he could.

He felt her other hand slide gently across his jaw, tugging his chin up until he had to look at her. Her gaze was intense, inescapable. He felt as if she had reached inside his head and started to rifle around, searching the scattered contents for some meaning or illumination.

"What are *you* thinking?" she asked in a raspy drawl.

He curled his hand behind her neck and pulled her closer. "How much I want to kiss you," he said, before he slanted his mouth over hers.

Something inside him let go as she curled her fingers around his shoulders and leaned into his embrace, her softer curves fitting snug against the harder edges of his own body.

Oh, hadn't he known she'd feel like this? Lush and hard and utterly right.

When he felt her tongue brush across his lips, he was lost. He opened himself to her kiss, deepened the caress until his heart was beating against his ribs like a caged animal, wild to be free. She let her hands roam up his neck to tangle in his hair, taking control with a thrilling show of confidence.

And when his cell phone started buzzing on the table beside them, it was Charlie who dragged her mouth away from his and took a step back, breaking the magic.

"Get it," she said hoarsely, moving several steps away.

He checked the display and sighed. "Hi, Mom," he answered.

"I just wanted to let you know I'm all settled in at the B and B."

"Good." He checked his watch and saw, to his dismay, that it was almost two o'clock. He was supposed to have met with Randall Feeney at two. In the chaos of the blitz attack at Charlie's place, and the false alarm of his mother's unexpected arrival, he'd forgotten all about it. "Mom, I've got to make a work call. Can I call you back later?"

"Of course. Talk to you soon."

"You were supposed to go see Randall Feeney," Charlie said after he'd hung up the phone. "What time?"

"About five minutes from now."

She tugged down her shirt, which he'd managed to displace during their kiss, and gave him a cool look. "Better get on the move. I know where to hide if the perimeter alarm goes off again."

He didn't want to go see Randall Feeney. He wanted to pull Charlie back into his arms and finish what they'd started.

But she had put up all her walls again, and maybe he'd do well to shore up his own, also. No matter how attracted he was to Charlie, he'd be a fool to forget the hidden dangers beneath her mirror surface.

And depending on what Randall Feeney had to say today, he just might learn a few things about Charlie he wasn't going to like.

WHEN MIKE STRONG laid on the smolder, he was downright lethal.

Charlie leaned her head back against the side of the guest room bed and looked at Nellie, who had ventured out from under the bed after Mike left and was sitting in front of Charlie, gazing back at her with solemn green eyes.

"He's a handful, Nels. A big, hunky handful."

Nearby, His Highness had curled into a ball and lay halfway between waking and slumber, his blue eyes blinking slowly at her.

"Don't judge me," she muttered. "A few hours ago, you had a cone on your head."

She definitely needed to cultivate a few human friends, she thought. Back during their teen years, she'd had Alice to share all her relationship troubles with, but Alice was gone. Had been gone for almost ten years now, and Charlie had never even tried to find a new best friend to whom she could tell her secrets.

Losing Alice had hurt too much for her to ever want to get that close to anyone else again.

Funny thing was, Charlie had always suspected that she was a lot more open with her thoughts and feelings with Alice than Alice ever had been with her. Alice had been far more worldly than Charlie, perhaps a result of growing up with money and social position, going to expensive adventure and learning camps in far-off places every summer while Charlie had been stuck in Bagwell, babysitting her cousin's brats for a little spending money and trying to steer clear of her brothers' latest crime sprees.

What was Randall Feeney going to tell Mike about her? she wondered. She couldn't imagine he'd have much good to say. The Beardens had been kind enough to her, from their safe position of social acceptability and comfortable wealth. Charitable, even.

No, Charlie thought with a shake of her head. That wasn't really fair, was it? Craig Bearden and his wife, Diana, had been genuinely kind and accepting of her.

At least, while Alice was alive.

But afterward…

Afterward, a lot of things had changed.

As for Randall Feeney, Charlie doubted he'd given much thought to her one way or another. He was Bearden's right-hand man, had been since Bearden had taken over the family law practice after his father's death. Feeney had been a young law clerk, and he'd become fast friends with Craig Bearden and even Diana, according to Alice.

She hadn't liked Feeney that much, Charlie remembered. Sometimes called him a toady, but Alice could be like that sometimes. Sharp-tongued when someone rubbed her the wrong way.

Feeney had apparently rubbed her the wrong way, though she hadn't really talked about him that much that Charlie could recall. Most of their conversations had been about the guys they'd crushed on in high school.

Alice had been the one who'd insisted on going to the public schools, headstrong from childhood. And as it had suited her father's political career to be seen as a man of the people rather than another rich fat cat, he'd agreed, though he might have come to regret that decision after Alice had become fast friends with a girl like Charlie.

Charlie pushed to her feet, the sudden movement sending Nellie scrambling for the space under the bed. She left the bedroom and headed into Mike's office, where her laptop was still plugged in, and checked her work email in hopes of a new project to tackle. But apparently nobody else wanted to work that weekend. All she found were a few spam emails and a couple of digests from one of the writing lists she subscribed to.

One of the messages was headed "What am I waiting for?" It was another member's rant at herself for putting off starting a new book. She'd received a rejection from an agent a few days before on a book that she'd sent just about everywhere in search of representation or publication. Now she was finding it hard to start something new rather than dwelling on her recent failures.

Which was still better than what Charlie was doing, which was avoiding starting anything at all.

For as long as she could remember, she had been a storyteller. Sometimes the stories had been crafted to stay out of trouble or to make her not-very-perfect life a little more palatable. Sometimes, her imagination just ran away with her, turning the ordinary into the fanciful because it entertained her and made her feel hopeful about the world.

But what she hadn't done in a long, long time was write a story down. Not since her college English teacher had told her she'd be smarter to focus on technical writing, where she'd be much more likely to find employment.

And she'd followed the advice, with good results. For the past six years, she'd managed to become a damn good technical writer.

But there were still stories running around in her brain, screaming to be heard.

When was she going to give them voice?

"What am I waiting for?" she murmured, staring at the laptop screen.

She switched programs, opening her word processor. The most recent file, besides the work-related documents, was titled "Alice."

She opened the Alice file and read the first line.

Two days before Christmas, nearly ten years ago, my friend Alice Bearden died.

She read the rest of the way through what she'd written, then she lifted her hands to the keyboard and continued.

Since that time, someone tampered with my brakes. Someone broke into my house and left a vivid message of destruction. A warning, perhaps, of what might happen if I keep trying to remember what happened the night of Alice's death?

Or is there someone else who might have a reason to want me dead?

Charlie sat back from the keyboard and stared at what she'd just written. She had a vivid imagination, it was true. But even she couldn't buy that she had some nameless, faceless tormentor out there, determined to terrorize her for no apparent reason.

Whatever was happening to her had to be about Alice's death. She wasn't high enough in the hierarchy at Ordnance Solutions to show up on the radar of anyone who might want to do harm to the company. She had very few friends or even acquaintances these days, much less enemies who would find her important enough to terrorize.

Everything went back to Alice and that night.

She erased the final line of her document, replacing it with a new sentence.

The only way to find out why someone has targeted me now is to return to the night Alice died. The memories of that night can't be gone completely. I'm remembering things now that, while I can't prove they're real, feel right to me. They make sense. They have a familiarity that tells me they're true.

So that's why tonight I'm going back to the place it all began.

The Headhunter Bar.

IT WASN'T RANDALL FEENEY who met Mike at the front door of the campaign office but the man himself, Craig Bearden. He looked remarkably like his head shots on the billboards and signs Mike had seen around Kentucky, from the white-toothed smile to the perfectly styled brown hair with just a touch of silver on the sideburns. His blue-eyed gaze was direct, and his handshake when he welcomed Mike into the office was dry-palmed and firm.

"I'm sorry you've gotten the runaround, Mr. Strong. May I call you Mike?"

"Certainly." Mike followed the man into a smaller office and discovered they were not alone. A tall, slim woman with tawny hair and sharp blue eyes was sitting on a small sofa in the corner of the room. She gave a nod as Mike entered.

"Mike, this is my wife, Diana. Diana, this is Mike Strong. He works at that new security agency in Campbell Cove."

"It's nice to meet you," Diana said, extending one long-fingered hand.

Mike shook her hand, then sat where Bearden indicated while the other man closed the door, shutting out the chatter of the busy campaign office.

"Mike, as you can imagine, Diana and I have had to deal with all sorts of people over the years interested in an emotional postmortem of my daughter's death. Some people can be vultures, I've learned, so I tend to be very cautious about whom I agree to talk to." Bearden took his seat behind his desk and folded his hands on the blotter in front of him. "But Becky

Cameron assured me you're not one of those people and said I should hear you out. So. Talk."

"I was expecting to meet with Randall Feeney," Mike began. "I wasn't expecting to speak directly with you and your wife."

"Does it matter?"

Of course it mattered. With Feeney, anything Mike asked wouldn't be a potential land mine the way it would be with Alice Bearden's parents. "I don't want to resurrect sad memories."

"They're not dead," Bearden said bluntly. "Grief doesn't die. It remains with you until *you* die."

"I'm sorry. Of course."

Diana Bearden waved her hand impatiently. "Don't feel you have to censor yourself. Ask what you want to know."

"Charlotte Winters is one of my students at Campbell Cove Academy." Mike watched Craig for any change of expression.

He was rewarded with a slight narrowing of Bearden's eyes. "Interesting. What kind of course?"

"Self-defense."

Diana Bearden's eyebrows lifted. "Charlotte Winters is quite able to take care of herself."

"She has good self-protective instincts," Mike said carefully.

"What about Charlotte directed you to me?" Bearden sounded curious. "Did she mention me to you?"

"No. We do background checks on students. To be certain their motives for taking part in our classes are what they say they are." That wasn't the truth, exactly—most of the students underwent a cursory check upon registration to make sure they didn't have outstanding warrants, but the kind of check he'd had Heller run on Charlie was out of the ordinary.

But the Beardens didn't need to know that.

"And our daughter's name came up." Bearden nodded slowly. "Alice and Charlotte were close. Perhaps too close."

"What do you mean?"

"Charlotte and our daughter came from different worlds," Diana said bluntly. "Perhaps that sounds elitist, but it doesn't make it untrue."

"Charlie was from a poor family."

"Not just poor," Craig said. "Unstable in a lot of ways. No father. A poorly educated mother with six small children to raise after his death. The children ran wild most of the time. There were discipline problems, especially with the two older boys. I suppose you know her two oldest brothers are in prison?"

"She said something about that, yes."

"That world was a world our daughter knew little about."

"Until she met Charlie?"

"Charlotte was different. I will grant you that. Unpolished, but very smart. She liked to please, and she wasn't afraid of working hard to get the things she wanted."

"I'm sensing a 'but' here," Mike murmured.

"Charlotte had a somewhat adversarial relationship with the truth."

Diana Bearden made a soft huffing sound, but when Mike glanced her way, her expression was unchanged.

Mike's stomach tightened. "She lies, you mean?"

"Not lies, exactly. *Augmentation* might be a somewhat better term," Craig suggested. "Charlotte starts with a kernel of truth, but she always seemed to find a way to make her reality bigger and better than it really was. For instance, her father didn't just die in a mining accident. He died saving a dozen other men."

"Did he?"

Bearden looked surprised by the question. "If he did, nobody ever spoke of it but Charlotte."

"Understandable, that she'd want to believe her father died a hero."

"Of course. But understanding a lie doesn't make it true."

"Charlie was with your daughter the night she died."

Bearden's lips tightened. "Yes."

"Do you blame her for it?"

Bearden didn't answer right away. The ache in the pit of Mike's stomach started to grow before the man finally spoke. "The person who ran over our daughter is to blame. The police assured me there was absolutely no evidence that Charlotte was that person. For one thing, I don't believe Charlotte had access to a vehicle at that time in her life."

"But if she had, do you think she was capable of leaving your daughter on the street to die?"

Again, Bearden's pause went on too long. "Do you?" he asked finally.

"I haven't known her long," Mike hedged.

"My gut instinct is no," Bearden admitted. "Charlotte might have been a fabulist, and she sometimes led Alice into situations that weren't good for either of them. But I never doubted her affection for our daughter. I don't think Charlotte would have left Alice to die."

The tension in Mike's gut started to ease. "I understand Charlie doesn't remember very much about your daughter's death."

"It seems the girls went out drinking at a bar in Mercerville." Diana Bearden clasped her hands more tightly in front of her. "They told us they were going to a movie that night."

"Not an uncommon thing for high school seniors to do, I suppose?"

"Not uncommon," Bearden agreed. "We just expected better judgment from our daughter. No matter what Charlotte wanted to do that night."

From what little Charlie had told him, it had seemed the idea to go to the bar had been Alice's, not Charlie's. But the Beardens had known the girl Charlie had been then. They'd also known their own daughter. Could Charlie be lying about what had really happened that night?

Or was she remembering only what she could allow herself to remember?

"I'm not sure we've given you the information you were looking for," Bearden murmured.

"You've both been helpful," Mike disagreed, though Bearden was right about one thing—they definitely weren't giving Mike the answers he was hoping for. They were just adding to the stack of unanswered questions piling up around the night of Alice's death.

And the more questions that arose, the more Charlie seemed to be in danger.

Bearden rose, as if he sensed this was the perfect time to bring the meeting to an end. "I've told Becky Cameron that we'll be happy to answer any of your questions in the future. I hope Diana and I haven't wasted your time today."

"On the contrary. I appreciate your time. I know this is a busy time for the two of you."

Diana remained seated on the sofa while Bearden walked Mike out to the sidewalk in front of the campaign office. He offered his hand.

Mike shook it. "Thank you."

"Charlotte wasn't a bad girl. And she's had almost ten years to grow up. I hear she's working as a technical writer for Ordnance Solutions."

So, Mike thought, Bearden had taken pains to keep up with his daughter's old friend. Interesting.

"Age and experience have a way of smoothing out the rough edges of a person's life," Mike agreed.

Bearden's expression darkened. "Alice never had that chance to grow."

Mike didn't know how to respond, so he just nodded and walked down the sidewalk to his truck, pulling out his phone as he slid inside the cab.

Charlie answered on the second ring. "How did it go?"

"It was interesting," he said vaguely.

"That's…unhelpful."

"Well, how about something I hope *will* help?"

"What's that?"

He put the keys in the ignition. "Put on your dancing shoes, darlin'. We're definitely going to the Headhunter Bar tonight."

Chapter Twelve

The Headhunter Bar hadn't changed in a decade. There were still kitschy fake shrunken heads hanging from the wall and a cheesy attempt at a tiki bar ambience complete with a straw-covered awning over the bar in the center of the room.

In contrast, the music was all Southern-fried classic rock—Lynyrd Skynyrd, the Allman Brothers, Marshall Tucker Band, the Doobie Brothers—blaring from large speakers in each corner of the room.

The sense of walking straight into the past sent goose bumps scattering across Charlie's skin. She paused in the entryway, trying to reorient herself to the world she'd left outside the bar, where she was a grown woman who had made a life for herself and not a nervous teenager with a fake ID burning a guilty hole in her pocket.

"Whose idea was it to come here that night?" Mike's voice barely carried over the driving beat of Lynyrd Skynyrd's "Gimme Three Steps," but it made her jump.

Mike put his hand on her arm, his fingers circling

her wrist and holding it lightly. The look in his eyes was somewhere between sadness and understanding.

"Alice's. Everything was always Alice's idea."

"And you did everything she suggested?"

Charlie shook her head. "Not everything. I had a well-honed instinct for survival. I knew there were things a rich girl could get away with that a poor kid from Bagwell never would."

"Illegal things?"

"Nothing terrible." Charlie nodded toward an empty table in the far side of the bar, far enough away from the speakers that they should be able to hear each other over the music.

Twining his fingers with hers, Mike led the way through the rough-looking Saturday-night crowd and pulled out her chair for her.

"You were saying, nothing terrible?" Mike sat across from her and leaned over the table to hear her better.

"Alice fancied herself a girl detective. Like Veronica Mars or something. She was always trying to solve things. I used to tease her that her life was too easy if she had to go looking for trouble to get into." She shook her head. "Finding trouble in Mercer County doesn't take much effort, you know?"

"Was she looking for trouble that night?"

"She was looking for something. She just never told me what." The déjà vu sensation was starting to get to her, making her head swim. Or maybe it was the loud music. Or the nearness of Mike Strong and his chiseled features and smoldering green eyes.

"Let's dance, okay?" She pushed up from her chair and headed for the dance floor, not waiting for him. The song had changed to a Little Texas ballad, slow enough for even Charlie, with her lack of dancing skills, to handle.

Mike caught up and wrapped one strong arm around her waist, drawing her close. "What are you afraid of?" he asked, his voice a rumble in her ear.

"This place," she said.

"What about it? The memories?"

She nodded, her forehead rubbing against his chin, the stubble of his beard rasping against the sensitive skin. "This place hasn't changed a bit. It's like walking into the past, and I didn't know how much that would affect me."

"I've got your back, you know. I'm not going to let anything happen to you tonight."

Oh, she wanted to believe him. Wanted to think that someone might actually be on her side for once.

The way Alice hadn't been. Not that night.

I'm sorry, Charlie. But I have to do the rest of this by myself.

"Alice came here for a reason, but she didn't tell me what it was. And she made sure I didn't know anything else about what she had planned."

"Made sure?" Mike repeated.

Charlie drew her head back and looked up at Mike, voicing the thought that had been creeping around the back of her mind since she first remembered Alice saying those words that night. "I think it was Alice who drugged my drink."

Mike was silent for a long time. The physical ease she was beginning to feel with him faded, and she started to tense up again, studying his face for signs that he thought she was crazy.

"Why would she do that?" He asked the question as if there could be a plausible answer. She started to relax again.

"I told you I've been having dreams about that night, right?"

He nodded.

"In one of the dreams, Alice said something odd. I clearly remember her saying 'I'm sorry, but I have to do the rest of this by myself.'"

His brow furrowed. "The rest of what?"

"I don't know!" Her voice rose in frustration. She lowered it quickly, not wanting to draw attention. "I told you she thought of herself as Veronica Mars, always looking for a mystery."

"You think she found one that killed her?"

"Yes. But I don't know what! She might have been my best friend, but I'm not sure I was hers."

"Was there someone else she might have confided in?" Mike asked.

"That's not really what I mean." The song was ending, but the temptation to stay in Mike's arms had a distracting effect. She couldn't seem to gather her thoughts to explain the kind of relationship she and Alice had shared.

Mike took her arm and steered her back to the table they'd vacated. A waitress came over from a nearby table. "What can I get you?"

"I'll take a ginger ale," Mike said. He looked at Charlie. "What's your poison?"

If she'd come here to relive that night, she should probably order another light beer. "Whatever light beer you have in a bottle."

The waitress jotted down the orders. "Want a menu?"

"Charlie?" Mike asked. She shook her head and he said, "Nothing, thanks," to the waitress.

After she left, he reached across the table and touched Charlie's hand. "You look ready to jump out of your skin."

She tried to shake off her nerves. "I'm sorry. I just— I haven't been back here since Alice died. I thought it would have changed a lot more than it has."

"You don't have to do this tonight if you're not ready." He hadn't released her hand, and the warmth of his fingers curled around hers had a settling effect on her, as if his strength were passing through his fingers into her own. "We can do this later. Or not at all."

"I've spent the past couple of days trying to think of anything else that might make someone want to hurt me." She turned her hand until her palm pressed against his. "And there's nothing else. My job can't be it. I don't have a boyfriend or a stalker ex."

"If what happened to Alice is what's behind the attacks on you, why now? It's been nearly ten years. Why would someone decide it's time to go after you now?"

"I think it's because I've started to remember things."

"Has something happened that would trigger your

memories?" His thumb had begun tracing circles across the skin of her wrist. The caress somehow managed to be both soothing and electrifying at the same time.

"I found a note from Alice a couple of weeks ago. It was stuck in an old Dickens novel I hadn't read since high school. I was having trouble sleeping, so I thought Dickens ought to do the trick," she added with a rueful smile. "It's so funny. Alice wasn't much of a note writer. She preferred phone or text or face-to-face communication. But she slipped a note into my book the day before she died, between classes. We were so close to graduating. Our lives were about to really begin."

"What did the note say?" Mike's voice had a gentle, coaxing tone, as if he understood how difficult it was for her to talk about her friendship with Alice and the night that led to her death. He was offering a kindness nobody else ever had, she realized. Certainly not the Beardens. Or her schoolmates, who'd never understood why pretty, popular Alice had taken one of those Winters kids under her wing. Not even Charlie's mother or her siblings, who had never felt comfortable with her running around with a Bearden. *Our people and her people just don't fit*, her mother had warned her, with genuine concern. *Nothing good will come of it.*

Maybe her mother had been right.

"It was our Christmas holiday," Charlie said, tightening her grip on Mike's hand. "School would start in a week, and then it would be a hard slog to graduation, with just spring break between us and the big bad world of adulthood. So Alice wrote me a note suggesting we needed to get a sneak peek at being grown-ups. The note told me to meet her outside her house at seven that night, and to be sure to dress to party."

"Are you sure it was from Alice?"

"I told you, she slipped the note in my book herself. Besides, she met me at the right place and time, as the note asked."

"I guess what I'm really asking is, are you sure the idea to come here was originally hers?"

"Oh." She thought about it. "I think it must have been."

"If she was going to drug you and ditch you, why invite you at all?"

"I don't know. For the longest time, I thought maybe she had been drugged, too, although nobody ever said so, not even when the police questioned me."

"They didn't think maybe you were drugged, too?"

She shook her head. "You'd have to understand where I came from. What my family was like. We were poor. Both my parents drank too much, and when they were drunk, they had a way of finding trouble. My two oldest brothers were mean drunks. In and out of jail all the time before they finally committed crimes they couldn't wriggle out of. When a Winters kid ends up passed out in the backyard and can't remember anything, it's not exactly a novel situation."

"But you didn't make a habit of that, did you?"

"No." She sighed. "But I think the cops always figured it was just a matter of time."

"They should have dug deeper." Mike sounded angry.

She gave his hand another squeeze. "Maybe they should have. But I get why they didn't."

"Take me through that night. Do you think you could walk me through what you remember? Where did you go when you entered the bar?"

She looked at the door, trying to recapture that moment in time. "The music was loud, just as it is now. Southern rock. A little country." She smiled a nervous smile at the memory, just as she had that night when they walked through the door. "Alice was wearing a short dress and a leather jacket with cowboy boots. Red snakeskin. All eyes turned to her. As always."

"Are you sure they weren't looking at you?"

She met Mike's eyes, relished the appreciation she saw there. "No, trust me. They were looking at Alice. I hadn't known how to dress, so I asked my brother. He told me to wear jeans and a sweater and I'd be fine. I think it was his way of trying to keep me out of too much trouble."

"I've seen you in a sweater," he murmured. "You're nothing but trouble in a sweater."

She flashed a smile. "Sweet talker."

"Did anyone approach y'all?"

Her smile faded. "Bees to honey. But Alice just swatted them all away. I just wandered along in her wake."

"Where did you sit?"

She nodded toward an empty table in the back of the room, close to the restrooms. "Right there, by that window in the back. She wanted to sit with her back to the wall, I guess so she could see the whole bar. I wondered at the time if she was looking for someone."

Mike nodded toward the table. "Go sit where you were that night. I'll let the waitress know we changed tables."

Charlie grabbed her purse and took a seat at the table in the back, shivering a little as snippets of memory flashed back to her. Alice's tawny hair had been pulled up in a messy ponytail at the crown of her head, wavy tendrils spilling over her cheeks and neck. She'd favored cat-eye makeup, with exaggerated liner that made her blue eyes look large and mysterious. She'd been smiling that evening. A lot. The kind of smile that said "I've got a secret and wouldn't you like to know?"

Charlie hadn't tried to coax her to spill the beans. By then, she'd known Alice well enough to realize that she couldn't be wheedled into anything she didn't want to do. Alice would tell her what was going on when she was good and ready.

And maybe she would have, if she hadn't been killed.

"Here we go." Mike's voice jarred her from the past. He set their drinks on the table in front of her and took the seat opposite. Immediately his eyes narrowed. "You look a little spooked."

"Alice was keeping a secret."

"Did she tell you that?"

"She didn't have to. It was written all over her face." Charlie looked at the small bottle of beer in front of her. Her stomach rebelled at the thought of taking a drink, but her throat was parched. She eyed Mike's ginger ale with envy before she forced herself to take a small sip of the beer. It was as bitter and unappetizing as she'd feared. She swallowed the sip quickly and pushed the bottle away.

"And you have no idea what that secret was?"

She shook her head. "I remember thinking that Alice would tell me when she was good and ready. But the evening never got that far."

"How do you think Alice drugged you?"

"She must have done it while I was in the bathroom. She stayed behind with our purses and the drinks."

"I thought women always went to the bathroom together." He smiled.

She managed a weak smile in return. "We do. In fact, I remember being a little surprised Alice didn't offer to go with me."

"And that was the only time she was alone with your drink?"

Charlie nodded. "I hadn't even taken a sip yet."

"And you don't remember anything after the first few sips of beer?"

She poked her fingernail at the coaster under her beer. "I had a dream the other night. Just a snippet of an image in time. I was lying on the ground, my cheek against the concrete. And across the street from me, Alice was lying there, too. In the street. One of her eyes was open but I knew she wasn't seeing anything." Charlie closed her eyes, but the image from her dream lingered in the darkness beneath her eyelids. She shuddered.

"You saw her when she was dead."

Charlie snapped her eyes open. "I must have. It seems so vivid now, like I was really there. But how?"

Mike drank half his drink before he spoke again. "When you woke up in your backyard, what did you do?"

"Sneaked back inside and crawled under my blankets. I was half frozen to death. I was lucky the weather didn't turn bitter that night, but it was December. Believe me, it was cold enough."

He frowned. "You were out in the elements for how long?"

"It had to be a few hours."

"Amazing you didn't have hypothermia."

"I was close. But where I woke was in a sheltered place. Under a juniper bush in the backyard. I guess maybe it was enough to shelter me from the worst of the cold."

"Still." Mike's frown deepened, carving lines in his face. "Whoever dumped you there couldn't have known you'd wake up before you lost too much of your body heat."

"You're saying whoever dumped me in my yard didn't care if I died."

"Or maybe thought you *would* die."

She wrapped her arms around herself, fighting off a shiver. "Whoever it was must have been surprised when I showed up alive."

"What did you think when you woke up with no memory of the previous night?"

"I was scared, obviously. And, to be honest, I was pretty embarrassed, too. I was supposed to be the Winters kid who didn't get drunk and pass out in the backyard."

"You didn't wonder how you got there?"

"Of course I wondered. I thought Alice must have delivered me home but forgotten to make sure I made it all the way inside. So I hurried inside, got into my pajamas and settled down in bed so I'd be there when Mama came to wake me up."

"Nobody was surprised when you didn't show up until morning?"

"No. I told Mama I'd be out late and not to wait up. She took me at my word." She rubbed her forehead, where a headache was starting to form. "I was the only kid in the family who never gave her any trouble. Well, not that kind of trouble, anyway."

The expression on his face suggested she'd piqued his curiosity. "What kind of trouble *did* you get into?"

"Little stuff. Lying, mostly. Harmless little lies to make my life seem better than it was. Lying so my teachers wouldn't know that my mom had been out all night drinking and hadn't had time to wash my jeans. I'd make up some kind of wild story about how I'd fallen in the mud that morning walking to the bus stop and hadn't had time to change before the bus came. Or make up some exotic ailment that kept me from showing up for school on days when Mama had to go out and couldn't take my little brother with her."

"What lie did you tell the morning after Alice's death?" Mike asked quietly, not sounding surprised by anything she was telling him. Did he already know about her reputation as a story fabricator?

"I told my mother that Alice and I had given each other makeovers, then fell asleep watching a movie."

"And she believed you?"

"Yes. I didn't lie to her. I mostly just lied about her."

She braced herself for the pity she feared she'd see in his eyes, but he merely nodded. "When did you find out what happened to Alice?"

"Around lunchtime. Someone from the high school started making calls to all the students because they were going to be setting up grief counselors on Monday and wanted us to know they'd be available." She smiled without mirth. "My mother was very surprised to learn that Alice had been killed in a hit-and-run when she was supposedly home in bed, tired out from a night of movie watching."

Mike took a sip of his ginger ale. "Did you tell her the truth?"

"I had to." Despite all the memories that had gone missing from that night, the images of the following day were vivid in her mind. She tugged at the collar of her shirt, starting to feel increasingly claustrophobic. "Could we get out of here? I really need to get out of here."

"Of course." Mike downed the rest of his ginger ale in one long gulp, then stood and pulled money from his wallet. He dropped a twenty on the table and helped her into her jacket. "You want to go home or do you want to look around outside, see if anything triggers your memories?"

She nodded toward the window next to the table. "See that alley out there? It leads down to Peavine Road. That's where Alice was found. I thought maybe if I went there, it might trigger more of that memory I had of seeing her body."

"Then let's go." He led her to the door, his hand settling against the base of her spine. There was a comforting heat in his touch, a hint of possessiveness, of staking his claim.

Or maybe that was the way it felt because that was how she was starting to think of him.

Her Mike. The stand-up guy who put himself on the line to protect her. Who looked at her with barely veiled desire in his green eyes. Whose fingers played lightly against her spine, sending shivers of answering desire through her body, despite her simmering tension.

She led the way to the alley, trying to focus her mind on the reason they'd come here in the first place. The narrow strip of gravel road was dark after the neon glow of the bar's front facade, forcing her to pick her way carefully through the broken glass and cigarette butts that littered the alley. Deep shadows, cast by the trees that grew haphazardly on the edge of the empty lot across the alley, shifted and writhed across the pathway.

It was quiet out here, too, the only sound the rattling tree limbs overhead, the muted bass line throbbing from inside the Headhunter Bar and the sound of their own breathing, quickening as they walked.

She found her gaze moving toward the empty lot. It hadn't been empty that night, she remembered. There had been a building there. One story. Cinder block. Looking closely, she could just see the remains of a foundation, almost hidden by the high grass.

They were nearing the end of the alley, where it fed into Peavine Road, when Mike's hand clutched suddenly at the back of her jacket. His weight toppled into her, pushing her down toward the ground. She landed hard on her shoulder and rolled until she lay with her cheek against the gritty dirt. Muddy yellow light bled onto Peavine Road from the streetlamp on the corner, and for a shuddering moment, she fully expected to see Alice's body lying broken and bleeding on the blacktop in front of her.

But the street remained empty. And the groaning sound that filled the silence came not from her own throat but from somewhere behind her. She rolled up to a sitting position, looking for the source of the noise.

She spotted Mike, lying in the gravel behind her. His eyes were open, but he seemed to have trouble focusing them.

She crawled to his side, ignoring the pain of

gravel biting into her palms and knees. "Mike, are you okay?"

Suddenly, his eyes rolled back into his head and his eyelids closed.

Chapter Thirteen

"No, Mike. Please don't do this to me!" Terrified, Charlie pressed her fingers to Mike's carotid artery and, with shivering relief, felt his pulse. But it seemed slow to her. His breathing, as well. And he didn't respond when she gave his shoulder a shake and said his name again.

She pulled her phone from her purse and dialed 911, trying not to panic. He'd been hit on the head earlier in the day. Had he sustained a closed head injury he hadn't realized?

Damn it, the phone wasn't ringing. She looked at her phone display and saw, to her dismay, that her battery was nearly dead.

"No no no! Mike?" She patted his cheeks. "Mike, wake up. Talk to me, please!"

His eyes opened briefly, and for a second, she thought he could see her. His mouth opened, a word escaping his lips on a whisper.

"Drug," he said. Then his eyes fell shut again.

Drug? What the hell? Had he taken something?

Had someone given him something, maybe spiked his drink in the bar? But why?

Look around you, Charlie, a voice murmured in the back of her mind. *You're all alone. Defenseless. No one could hear you if you screamed, not over that noise in the bar.*

And Mike wasn't able to save her this time.

The night air seemed to chill by several degrees, making her shiver uncontrollably. She reached into Mike's pocket in search of his phone, but it wasn't in either of his front pockets. She started to roll him over but stopped herself, realizing he might have injured his spine when he fell. If she moved him now, it could make his injuries worse.

But she needed a damn phone! If he was wrong, if his head injury was worse than he'd thought, there could be blood filling his brain and killing him right now.

"I've got to go find help, but I'll be right back," she told him, reaching out to brush his hair away from his forehead. "I promise."

She pushed to her feet and started walking unsteadily on the gravel path back to the bar's well-lit facade. But before she made it halfway, a shadow moved across the rectangle of light slanting across the end of the alley.

It was a man. He was dressed in dark clothes, barely perceptible in the gloom. Dark jeans, a long-sleeved top that seemed to have a hood. His features wouldn't have been easy to make out in the low light as it was, but the shadows from the hood rendered his face nothing but a black oval, devoid of all light.

He didn't speak. Didn't call out to ask if everything was okay. He just stood there, silent and terrifying.

Then he took a step toward her. Then another.

She backpedaled, almost losing her balance as her feet skidded across the loose gravel. She turned and ran, fighting the urge to try to grab Mike's body and drag him along behind her.

She couldn't help Mike by getting hurt herself. She needed to get back to the crowded bar, where there would be safety in numbers, and get some of the patrons to help her.

Reaching the end of the alley, she twisted to her left to head up the side street to the front of the bar. But the second she rounded the corner, she ran headlong into a solid obstacle.

Hands grabbed at her arms, holding her still when she tried to jerk away. Panic was scrambling her brains, but she somehow remembered to use her weight to her advantage. Dropping her shoulder, she rammed into her captor, hitting him somewhere between his stomach and his upper thighs. He expelled air with a pained growl, twisting aside, a move that sent her sprawling to the pavement.

For a moment, she felt as if she were trapped in one of her dreams about Alice's death, the one where she was lying on the pavement, looking across the road to where Alice lay bloody and dead.

But there was no Alice tonight. Only the pained panting of the man whose clutches she'd just escaped.

She scrambled up from where she'd fallen and started to run. But a hand snaked out and grabbed her elbow, jerking her backward again.

As she started to struggle again, a familiar voice gasped, "For God's sake, Charlie, stop it. It's me."

She stopped fighting and stared up into the flint-gray eyes of Deputy Archer Trask.

"What are you doing?" she asked, her voice rising. "Why are you here?"

"I could ask you the same question. Imagine my surprise when I spotted you and Mike Strong walking into the Headhunter Bar. Not exactly a place I ever thought you'd visit again, under the circumstances—"

"Mike!" she said, panic starting to wane enough for her brain to start functioning again. "You've got to help me, Trask. Mike's in the alley. He's passed out—I don't know why. He got hit on the head earlier today, but he said he never lost consciousness, and he hasn't been acting strange, so I don't know if it's that or if maybe someone spiked his drink. Wait!" she added as he started to move toward the alley. "There was someone else in the alley. He didn't say anything, didn't ask if Mike was okay. I think— I think he was following us. Do you have your gun?"

Trask pulled a pistol from inside his jacket. "Stay here."

"Be careful!"

She pressed her back against the side wall of the bar, feeling the thud of the music throbbing through the brick behind her. Her heart was tripping along at light speed, making her feel light-headed and queasy.

A moment later, she heard Trask call her name. "It's clear," he called.

She hurried back into the alley to find Trask crouched beside Mike's body, the beam from a small flashlight illuminating part of the scene. "Is he still breathing?" she asked.

"Seems to be. His pulse is pretty slow, though." Trask flashed the light around the alley. "I didn't see anyone when I got here."

"He was there, Trask. I didn't make him up."

Trask looked up at her. "I didn't say you did. He might have heard the commotion we were making and run the other way. Do you think he was after you or Mike?"

"I don't know. Maybe me. Or maybe I read the whole thing wrong. I'm a little on edge, and when the guy didn't say anything at all…"

On the ground at her feet, Mike's head rolled from side to side, as if he were trying to shake off the effect of the drug and return to consciousness. He mumbled something that sounded like her name, then fell still again.

"My phone battery's dead. We need to call 911."

Trask pulled out his phone. "I'll call it in. Don't move. I have more questions."

Of course he would, she thought. She knew he'd never really been happy with the official story about what happened to Alice. Trask had always thought it was a little too convenient that Charlie said she couldn't remember anything that happened that night after her first few sips of beer.

Trask returned to where she crouched beside Mike, stroking his hair. "Paramedics are on the way."

"Thank you."

"What about you? You feeling woozy or anything? How much did you drink?"

"One sip of beer. I'm fine. I think maybe the idea was to get Mike out of the way so I'd be vulnerable."

"To who?"

"That's the question." She rubbed her forehead, where a dull ache had formed above her eyes. "I don't know. That's why we came here, to see if I could piece anything together."

"Piece what together?" Trask asked, his tone wary.

She made herself meet his flinty gaze. "What really happened the night Alice died."

AMELIA STRONG PACED the waiting room floor, her pale face creased with worry. Charlie watched her for a few seconds, swamped with guilt, before Archer Trask walked back into the waiting room with two cups of coffee, drawing her attention away from Mike's mother.

Trask gave Amelia one of the cups, then brought the other to the chair where Charlie sat. He took the seat next to her, inclining his head when she thanked him.

"Still nothing from the doctors?"

She shook her head. "I think they were taking him for a CT scan first, to be sure it's not a closed head injury. They're also going to do a tox screen to rule out the usual drugs, but I don't think they'll find anything."

"I asked them to do a urine test for GHB," Archer said quietly.

She looked up at him. "So you *do* think he was drugged."

"I want to rule it in or out," Trask said carefully.

"I think I was drugged the night Alice died."

Trask's eyes narrowed a notch.

"I remember almost nothing from that night. I took three sips of beer that I remember, and then the night is mostly a blank until I woke up in my backyard."

"Mostly?" Trask turned toward her. "You remember something?"

She wished now that she'd never told Trask what she and Mike had been doing at the Headhunter Bar. She should have known he'd immediately think the worst of her, put the most damning possible spin on what she had been doing.

"Is this an interrogation?" she muttered.

"No, I just—" Trask cut off whatever he'd been going to say when a thin black man in green scrubs entered the waiting room and headed for Amelia Strong.

"Mrs. Strong?" the doctor asked as Amelia stopped pacing and turned to watch his approach with anxiety-filled eyes. "I'm Dr. LeBow. I've been treating your son."

"Is he going to be okay?" Amelia asked, reaching her hand toward Charlie.

Charlie caught Amelia's hand and gave it a squeeze.

Trask moved up to stand on her other side. She quelled a grimace.

"The good news is, the CT scan didn't show any sort of brain injury, and the cut on his forehead seems to have caused only minor bruising and minimal swelling." Dr. LeBow's deep voice was calm and reassuring. "The tox screen came back negative, but the urine test Deputy Trask requested came back positive for gamma hydroxybutyric acid. It was probably ingested shortly before he lost consciousness."

"So how do you treat something like that?" Amelia asked.

"For a GHB overdose, we primarily offer supportive care—he's breathing on his own, but if his respirations dip to a critical point, we can intubate and breathe for him until the drug is out of his system."

Charlie's heart squeezed at the thought of Mike on life support, all because he was trying to help her. "Do you think you'll have to do that?"

"At this point, no. He's already starting to show signs of waking, so we'll continue to monitor his vitals. He's fit and, from what you've told us and we've observed, in good health. He has an excellent chance of full recovery with no lingering effects." He lowered his voice, even though there were no other people in the waiting room at the moment. "Has this ever happened to Mr. Strong before? Is he a recreational drug user?"

"No," Amelia snapped. "Of course not."

"He wasn't using drugs tonight," Charlie said firmly. "I was with him from about five o'clock on, and the only time he left my sight was tonight at the bar, when he picked up our drinks from the waitress. He was drinking ginger ale. I believe someone spiked it."

Dr. LeBow looked mildly skeptical. "I see."

"It can't be the first time you've treated someone who was roofied," Charlie said, not quite able to hide her annoyance.

"No, but the victim is usually female." Dr. LeBow glanced at Trask. "I'm going to have to get back to my other patients. We're moving Mr. Strong to ICU until we're satisfied that he's awake and able to maintain his respiration and blood pressure without intervention. The waiting room for ICU is on the fourth floor. Let the nurse know you're there and she'll let you visit him for a short time."

Amelia followed the doctor out of the room. As Charlie started to follow, Trask caught her arm.

"What?" she snapped.

"We weren't finished talking yet. You know you won't get to see him right away, so what does it hurt to hear me out?" He nodded toward the seats they'd recently vacated. "I promise, I'll go upstairs with you when we're done and make sure you're allowed to see him if you'll stay here and finish answering my questions. Deal?"

She sighed, frustrated and anxious. She knew he was right, even if she didn't want to admit it. She wasn't family. In most people's eyes, she'd barely qualify as a friend. Archer might be her best hope of getting to see Mike again tonight at all.

And maybe it was time to bring Archer Trask in on what she was beginning to suspect about Alice's death. Her murder had been his first case as an investigator. If he had lingering doubts her death was anything but a hit-and-run accident, then he had almost as much incentive as Charlie had to get to the truth.

She sat in the waiting room chair and folded her hands on top of her knees, waiting for him to sit, as well.

He pulled one of the chairs around to face her and took his seat. "What have you remembered about that night, Charlie?"

Slowly, carefully, she told him about her dreams. "I know you're thinking they're just dreams. My imagination running ahead of me. But I think they're real."

"So you were there on the street that night that Alice was killed."

"I think so. And I think the reason I can't remember much of that night is that I was drugged, just like Mike was tonight."

Trask's eyes narrowed. "Who drugged you?"

This, she knew, was the part that would be hard for anyone else to believe. But she had to say it.

"I think it was Alice."

Trask stared at her for a moment. "Why would you think that?"

"I had a memory of hearing Alice talk to me when I was barely awake. She said, 'I'm sorry, but I have to do the rest of this by myself.'"

"Do you know what she meant?"

She shook her head. "But she was being really

mysterious about something. She did that, sometimes. Went all Trixie Belden on me."

"Trixie Belden?"

"Books Alice and I read when we were kids. Trixie Belden, girl detective. Or maybe Alice was emulating Veronica Mars or something. She just liked to solve puzzles. Sometimes, she stuck her nose where it didn't belong, and the people at school would get mad at her." Charlie smiled grimly. "They couldn't stay mad, though. Alice had a way about her."

"Yeah, that's the picture I got of her, too."

Charlie looked at Trask through narrowed eyes, feeling as if she might be getting her first real glimpse of the man behind the badge. He hadn't been that much older than her and Alice when he caught the hit-and-run case. Midtwenties at most. Which put him in his midthirties now, around the same age as Mike. Funny how much older he'd seemed ten years ago.

"You never thought it was just a hit-and-run, either, did you?" she asked.

He held her gaze a moment without speaking. Then he looked down at his hands, which twisted together almost nervously between his parted knees. "No. I didn't."

"I thought you suspected me. Am I right?"

"You were a person of interest," he admitted. "Of course. You were there with her that night. You disappeared. You claimed you couldn't remember anything that happened and you couldn't account for your whereabouts between eight that night and four the following morning."

"When you put it that way…" she murmured.

"You didn't exactly cooperate."

"When you're a Winters, it doesn't pay to cooperate with the police." She tried out a wry smile.

He answered it with a quirk of his lips. "Fair enough."

"Do you believe me about that person I saw in the alley tonight?" she asked, a little afraid of how he'd answer.

"Yeah, I believe you."

"Even without seeing him?"

"I sent an officer to ask around the bar after we left," he said. "I gave him your description of the man you saw. The clothing, the build, the general impression that he was young and fit. Three people at the bar remembered seeing a man in a hoodie come in not long after you and Mike. One of the officers is watching the bar's surveillance video to see if he can spot the guy."

"I didn't even think about security video." She rubbed her gritty eyes. "I didn't think about anything but what was happening to Mike. I wish I'd never gotten him involved in all this."

"If I know anything about Mike Strong, I doubt you could have stopped him from getting involved if it was something he wanted to do." Trask sighed, frustration beginning to show in his sharp eyes. "Don't you think it's weird that you were drugged in this bar ten years ago, and now you're there again and your buddy Mike gets slipped a mickey?"

"Yes. And what if it's connected?"

Trask's eyes narrowed. "You said Alice drugged you."

"Yeah, I think she did. Her father had warned her and me both about date rape drugs before he let Alice go to any parties. And as curious as Alice was, I can easily see her finding out where to get her hands on GHB or something like that if she thought it would be helpful to whatever she was investigating."

"Investigating," he said skeptically.

"Trixie Belden, remember?" She looked at Trask. "Can't we talk about this later? I really need to see Mike. I need to see for myself that he's getting better."

Trask's expression softened and he rose to his feet. "So let's go see what we can do."

Chapter Fourteen

Mike could hear a steady cadence of beeps and the occasional sound of voices in quiet conversation in the distance. The ringing of a phone. A voice over what sounded like an intercom. A medicinal tang filled his nose when he breathed, giving him a vague sense of unease.

Something was wrong. He couldn't seem to open his eyes. He couldn't move. He knew he wasn't where he was supposed to be, but he didn't know where he was.

"Mike?" Her voice sliced through the haze in his brain, and he latched onto it like a lifeline.

Charlie.

"Can you hear me, Mike?" She sounded worried. Afraid. That wasn't the way Charlie was supposed to sound. Charlie was snappy comebacks and whistling in the dark.

"I need you to wake up, Mike. Please. I need to know you're going to be okay."

For you, Charlie, he thought, *I'll crawl through glass.*

His eyelids felt like lead weights, but he made

himself open them. The world spun a few times before coming to a stop, and he finally got a look at his surroundings.

Hospital. ICU, maybe. Lots of monitors, lots of annoying beeps. There was a nasal cannula pouring oxygen into his nose and a blood pressure cuff folded around his right arm. A clip on his finger measured his blood oxygen level.

And standing next to him, her face pale but her hair a shock of color in the otherwise drab room, was Charlie Winters, gazing at him with a quivering smile on her lips.

"Hey," he said, his voice coming out raspy.

"Hey." Her smile widened, and it was as if the sun had come out to dazzle him. "Do you know where you are?"

"Either the worst hotel room in the world or the hospital. What happened?"

Her smile faded. "You don't remember anything, do you?"

"No." He grimaced, lifting his hand to his head, which had started to ache behind his eyes. His fingers touched a bandage on the side of his head.

Right. The assailant in Charlie's house.

When had that happened? It seemed like just a few minutes ago, but he'd been able to go home, hadn't he? He'd gone home because Charlie needed him.

Hadn't he? But why had she needed him?

"Was my head injury worse than I thought?" He was starting to worry now. Why couldn't he remember anything? He tried to think past the run-in with the man at Charlie's, but everything seemed to be a blank.

"No." Charlie took his hand in hers. Her fingers were cold, but her grip was tight. "Do you remember anything about last night?"

"Last night?" He frowned. "What time is it?"

"It's about three thirty in the morning. You're in the hospital."

"I don't understand."

"We went to the Headhunter Bar. Do you remember anything about that?"

That's right. They had planned to go to the bar that evening. He'd gone to see Randall Feeney and ended up talking to Craig Bearden.

But what had happened after that?

"What happened to me, Charlie?"

"The best I can tell, someone drugged your drink at the bar."

"At the Headhunter?"

Her thumb was doing all kinds of distracting things to the inside of his wrist. He had to exert a lot of mental effort in order to focus on what she was saying. "We ordered drinks. You had a ginger ale. I had a beer. You drank the whole glass of ginger ale pretty quickly, which is probably why it hit you so fast and hard."

"Did I pass out in the bar?" It was stupid to feel embarrassed by the idea, since he'd done nothing wrong. But still, he didn't like the idea of face-planting in front of a bunch of strangers.

"No, you fell down outside. We were going to see if the road where Alice died would jog my memory."

"Did it?"

"We didn't get that far." She bent closer, near enough that her clean, crisp scent managed to mask even the sharpest of medicinal smells in the hospital room. He breathed her in, let the heady scent of her fill his lungs. "Mike, I'm so sorry. I'm sorry I ever got you involved in any of this."

He reached up and touched her face, ignoring the painful tug of the IV cannula in the back of his hand. "I'm not sorry. Not about trying to protect you, trying to get to the bottom of what's happening to you. So wipe that guilty look off your pretty face and give me a smile."

She managed a weak smile. "Better?"

"Much. Who else is here?"

"Your mom," she answered. "And Deputy Trask was here for a while, but he went home to get some sleep. He said he'd be back in the morning."

"Archer Trask? From my class?"

"He was at the bar last night. He was a big help when you passed out."

There was something she wasn't telling him, he thought, but he didn't feel clearheaded enough to call her on it. He'd get it out of her later. "Have you called anyone from my office?"

She shook her head. "Everything's been so crazy here, waiting for you to wake up. Do you want me to call one of them?"

"Call Maddox Heller. Tell him what's happened. And then get him to come pick up you and my mom and take you to my place. Tell him I want someone to stay there with you until I'm released."

He had expected her to argue, but she simply inclined her head and said, "Okay."

Now he knew there was something going on that she wasn't telling him.

"They're going to kick me out of here any minute, so do me a favor and get better, fast. Okay?"

"Count on it."

At that moment, a nurse entered. "Well, look who's awake."

"Hope I haven't been too much trouble," Mike said. "Have I been here long?"

"A few hours. But your vitals have been improving steadily." The nurse looked at Charlie, her expression sympathetic. "I'll need you to skedaddle for a bit. Someone will let you know when Mr. Strong can have a visitor again. Meanwhile, why don't you try to get some sleep. You don't want to end up in here yourself."

Mike held on to Charlie's hand when she tried to slip away. "Call Heller. And talk my mother into going home with you."

She bent and kissed his forehead. "Try not to rush this getting-better thing, okay? Do what the nurses and doctors tell you. I'll be in touch soon."

He watched her leave, wanting to ask her to stay with a desperation that caught him by surprise. He wasn't a guy who formed attachments easily. Life as a Marine had been a life constantly on the move, from base to base or battlefront to battlefront. He'd connected to his band of brothers with all the instant camaraderie of war, but romantic entanglements had been short-term affairs, no strings, with women who understood the score. But what was happening between him and Charlie felt different. Long-term and intense.

Permanent? Maybe.

He'd never thought of a relationship outside his family as permanent before. Could what he was feeling for Charlie be different?

He had to get out of this hospital bed, he decided as the nurse finished taking his vitals. He needed to get back to Charlie. It was his job to keep her safe. His job to help her unravel the hidden secrets of her past.

He'd be damned if he was going to hand it off to anyone else.

"WHAT DO YOU THINK?" Archer Trask asked, his voice tense.

Charlie peered at the video on the computer screen, trying to make out the fuzzy images on the security video. "He's the right size, and the hoodie looks right. But the picture's pretty awful."

"It's the best we could do." Trask sighed.

"I know. I'm sorry. I just didn't get a good look at him. He was basically a silhouette, and I didn't see his facial features at all."

"It was a long shot at best." He took the flash drive out of her computer and put it back in its evidence bag, which he stashed in his jacket pocket. He nodded at the open doorway, where Maddox Heller was standing guard. "What's going on with the muscle?"

Charlie saw Heller's lips quirk in a half smile. "He's keeping an eye on Mrs. Strong and me until Mike comes home."

Trask leaned against the window and cocked his head. "What aren't you telling me, Charlie? You and Strong go to the bar where you and Alice spent her last night on earth, and he ends up in the hospital with a GHB overdose. Then he sends a bodyguard to watch you and his mother until he can get home. Does he think you're a target or something?"

"I think maybe we're both targets now," she admitted.

"When did this start?"

"Well, for me, I started getting the feeling I was being watched or followed a few weeks ago, after I started having the dreams about Alice's death. I tried to contact Craig Bearden, to see if he'd talk to me, but he never returned my call."

"What kind of message did you leave?"

"I told him I thought I was remembering things about that night, and I wanted to talk to him about it."

Trask's gray eyes narrowed. "And he never called back?"

"That's weird, isn't it?" Charlie worried her lower lip between her front teeth. "You'd think if there was anything new about the case, he'd want to know about it. But he never called, never sent an email or anything."

"Maybe he didn't get the message. Did you leave it at home or at his office?"

"His office."

"Maybe someone retrieved the message before he did and forgot to give it to him."

"Or maybe he just thinks I'm a big, fat liar who got his daughter killed," she muttered, looking down at her hands. They had started twisting together of their own volition, a telltale sign that she was feeling anxious and self-conscious. She stilled her hands, clutching them together tightly in her lap. "Anyway, after that, I started getting the weirdest feeling that I was being watched. You know, when you get that creeping sensation down the back of your neck when someone's staring at you? But I never saw anyone."

"Is that why you decided to take the self-defense course?"

"Yes. And then, two days later, someone tampered with the brakes of my car."

Trask pushed away from the window abruptly. "What?"

"My brake line was cut and the fluid drained out while I was at my self-defense class. If Mike hadn't seen the puddle of fluid where my car had been and realized I was in trouble..." She told him about her brakes failing and the way Mike had stopped her car before it crashed. "He saved my life."

"What a stroke of luck. How'd he happen to know whose car the brake fluid came from?"

She frowned at his suspicious tone. "He was watching me leave."

"So, you were being watched by both some unknown person *and* Mike Strong? All in one week?"

"Go to hell, Trask." She stood up and walked toward the door.

Trask caught her arm, his grip gentle. "Sorry. I'm a cop. Suspicious is my middle name. Finish telling me what else happened. Why are you staying here? Because of the brake tampering?"

"No. We sort of blew that off. The guy at the garage couldn't say for sure how the line was cut at the time. So Mike sent it to the security agency for his people to take a closer look. But then I walked into my house a day later after self-defense class and discovered my place had been trashed." She told him about the vandalism and about Mike's decision that she needed a safer place to stay until they could figure out who was messing with her.

"Did you think to call the police?"

"Yes, actually. Officer Bentley of the Campbell Cove Police Department wrote up a report for my insurance company, but he told me that since nothing was stolen, I'd do better to spend my time getting as much insurance reimbursement as my policy would allow."

"He's probably right," Trask admitted. He folded his arms over his chest, looking thoughtful. "What happened to Strong's head? Did that have anything to do with what's going on with you?"

"We think so."

After she finished telling him about the intruder at her house the previous day, he shook his head. "You know, you could have called me if you thought any of this was connected to Alice's death."

She stared up at him with disbelief. "Trask, you treated me as if I was your prime suspect in Alice's death. Why on earth would I go to you with any of this?"

He sighed again. "Fair enough. I hope you realize now that I'll hear you out. We're on the same side, Charlie. I want to find out what really happened to Alice that night, too."

"Then we need to find whoever trashed my house and tampered with my brakes and drugged Mike."

A small commotion coming from the front of the house drew Trask's attention away from Charlie. He headed out of the room, Charlie on his heels. Maddox Heller, who'd been standing guard outside the office, brought up the rear. They reached the living room to find Amelia Strong engulfing her son in a bear hug.

"Why didn't you call me?" Amelia asked. "I'd have come to pick you up myself."

"I needed Eric's medical degree to talk the doctors into springing me early," Mike answered, gently disentangling himself from his mother's arms. He met Charlie's gaze and smiled, but his expression faded into suspicion when he caught sight of Archer Trask. "Deputy, what a surprise to see you."

"Charlie was catching me up on everything that's been happening to you." Trask crossed to where Mike stood and extended his hand. "I think we all want the same thing. For Charlie to be safe and to find out what really happened to Alice."

Mike hesitated a moment, his gaze slanting toward Charlie once more. She gave a little nod, and he reached out and shook Trask's hand. "Charlie tells me I have you to thank for getting me to the hospital so quickly."

Trask looked at Charlie. "Don't thank me. Charlie was the one who risked her life to help you."

Mike's gaze snapped back to Charlie. "Risked her life?"

Trask looked at her as well, one eyebrow raised.

"I haven't really had a chance to tell Mike everything that happened that night," Charlie said. "And I wouldn't say I exactly risked my life. I ran for help. That's all."

"What the hell were you running from?" Mike asked.

"Language," Amelia murmured, making everybody in the room chuckle, even Mike.

"Mrs. Strong, why don't we go to the kitchen and fix some sandwiches for everybody," Maddox Heller suggested, gently steering Amelia away from Mike. He looked over at Deputy Trask. "Trask, you can help us by putting ice in glasses."

Within a few seconds, the living room was empty except for Mike and Charlie. She ventured a smile, but he didn't return it. Instead, he crossed to where she stood, took her hand and pulled her with him down the hall to the spare bedroom.

He closed the door behind them and caught her

up in his arms, slanting his mouth hard against hers. Caught off guard, she clung to him for balance as the world around her started to spin like a top.

There was nothing gentle about this kiss. It was pure fire, burning her to her core until she felt as if she were nothing but ashes. Then the flames roared again and she rose from the ashes to burn as his mouth traced a path of fire along the curve of her cheek and down the side of her throat.

As if something inside her had snapped, she felt released from shackles, free to be the person she had always wanted to be. Free to take the things she wanted most without fear or shame.

And what she wanted most, she realized, was Mike Strong. His strength. His laughter.

His lips gliding slowly, deliberately toward the curve of her breasts, where they peeked from the collar of her shirt.

When he drew back, it happened so suddenly that her knees started to buckle. He wrapped his arm around her and pulled her over to the bed, where he sat, bringing her down onto his lap.

"Okay," he said in a shaky voice, "before we get too carried away, there's something I need to know. You know, last night, when I woke up, I knew you were keeping something from me. So how about you tell me exactly what you were running from in the alley."

Chapter Fifteen

When Charlie and Mike entered the kitchen, where Trask and Heller waited, Heller pulled Mike aside. "On a hunch, I checked your truck. There had to be some way Charlie's stalker has been tracking y'all without your noticing the tail."

"I would hope so."

"Well, I was right. You picked up a rogue GPS tracker at some point. I've left it there for now."

"Why?"

Heller just nodded for Mike to join him as he crossed to the kitchen table, where Charlie had taken a seat.

"I don't like hiding." Charlie's voice was low and composed, but Mike had begun to understand her well enough to see the barely restrained restlessness lurking behind her eyes as she looked up to meet his gaze. It wasn't just the hiding that was getting to her. She was done with being a target.

"Until we know who's after you, keeping you hidden is the best way to keep you safe." Archer Trask crossed to the empty chair at the table where Charlie sat and leaned toward her. His attitude toward Charlie had changed, Mike noted. On one hand, Mike was glad for Charlie to have a few more people on her side. On the other hand, Trask had just taken the chair Mike had been about to claim for himself. And the warmth in Trask's eyes was really beginning to annoy him.

"So let's figure out who's after me, then," Charlie said, a hint of frustration beginning to seep into her voice. "It has to be connected to whatever happened the night Alice died, doesn't it?"

"I think so," Maddox Heller agreed. "You said the sensation of being watched or followed started shortly after you left a message at the Craig Bearden for Senate campaign office, right?"

"Yes." Charlie looked at Mike, her eyes expressive. She was tired of going over all the details of her story, and he sympathized with her annoyance, but her story was all they had to go on at the moment. And what they knew was limited by how very little she remembered.

"Have you ever considered undergoing hypnosis?" Mike asked.

Trask gave him a sharp side-eye glance.

"You think I'd remember more under hypnosis?" Charlie asked, her tone skeptical. "I don't think drug-related amnesia is something you can counteract with mind games."

"No, but if there weren't any more memories to retrieve, I'm not sure you'd be remembering new details in your dreams."

Charlie pushed to her feet, the chair legs making a loud screeching sound against the floor. She paced the kitchen floor, raking her hair out of her eyes with her fingers. "What if those aren't really memories? What if everything I think I'm remembering is just something I'm making up in my head to fill in all those awful blanks?"

Mike planted himself in front of her and gently closed his hands around her upper arms. "Do you think it's something you're making up?"

She closed her eyes a moment, her brow furrowed. Then her eyes snapped open and she shook her head. "No. I think they're really memories."

"Then that's what we go with." Mike turned to look at the other two men. "Agreed?"

"Agreed," Trask said.

Heller nodded. "It would probably help if we could access more of your memories."

"Do either of you know anyone who uses hypnosis to recover memories?" Mike asked.

"It's not considered a reliable way to remember things," Trask warned. "People tend to remember things that aren't real if the hypnotist leads them at all. Especially people already prone to confabulation."

"Meaning me," Charlie murmured to Mike.

"Lauren Pell is a trained psychiatrist," Heller said. He looked at Mike. "She works in our PSYOPS training division."

"Can we get her here fast?" Mike asked.

"I'll find out." Heller pulled out his phone.

Mike cupped Charlie's elbow and pulled her aside.

"You don't have to do this if you don't want to. We can find another way."

Charlie shook her head. "I need to do this. Even if the idea scares me."

He brushed a floppy lock of hair away from her forehead. "Why does it scare you?"

"If there are memories I can retrieve, if it's not drug-related memory loss, why haven't I remembered any of this for ten years? What if I saw something that I don't want to remember?" Tears welled in her eyes, and she blinked hard to keep them from falling. "What if I did something I don't want to remember?"

Mike looked across the room at Trask, who sat with one foot propped on the opposite knee, watching them curiously. He lowered his voice further. "You were investigated as a person of interest. If there was anything to tie you to what happened to Alice, I have every reason to believe you'd have been charged."

"I didn't kill her," she said. "But what if I did something to put her in that situation?"

"I'll tell you the same thing Craig Bearden told me. The only person to blame is the person who ran over Alice. Nobody else."

"He said that?"

"He did."

That earned him a smile from her. "There was a time when I thought Mr. and Mrs. Bearden actually liked me. They were both always really kind and accepting of my friendship with Alice. But after she died..."

"Death has that effect on people."

"I know." She stepped closer, until her warmth washed over him, and leaned her forehead against his shoulder. "It had a similar effect on me."

Heller's voice interrupted. "Lauren's on her way. She suggests that we all clear out except for Charlie and Mike. She'd like to keep the distractions to a minimum."

Trask stood and stretched. "I'll head back to the station and see if there's anything there that needs my attention. Call if you need me. And be sure to record that session."

He followed Heller down the hallway to the front door. Mike and Charlie trailed after them, Mike locking the door behind the two men before turning back to Charlie. She gazed back at him, worry lines creasing her forehead.

"It's gonna be okay, Charlie. I'm not going to let anything happen to you."

She closed the distance between them, walking into his outstretched arms. "I know. And thank you."

"We have a lot to talk about, you and me," he murmured against her hair. "You know that, don't you?"

She nodded, her hair sliding like silk against his cheek. "I know. But I just can't think about anything like that right now. Do you understand?"

"Yeah," he said, although her reluctance sent a little flutter of anxiety through his chest. What if she didn't want to pursue what they felt for each other? What if she didn't feel the same way he was beginning to feel?

Later, he told himself. *Worry about it later.*

Right now, protecting Charlie was the only thing that mattered.

CHARLIE WASN'T SURE she was really under hypnosis. She felt very aware of her surroundings, of the soft, soothing voice of the hypnotherapist Lauren Pell. She was a tall woman in her thirties, with short dark hair, soft blue eyes and a gentle manner that had made Charlie feel instantly at ease.

"Tell me about the taste of the beer," Lauren suggested. "Was it cold or lukewarm?"

"Lukewarm," Charlie answered, grimacing as she spoke. "And bitter. I remember wishing I'd gotten a drink like Alice's. Hers looked so good, but I was afraid of trying anything with hard liquor in it. Alice teased me about it. Said I was a big chicken."

"Did that make you angry?"

"No." Charlie smiled. "I was a big chicken. But I also wasn't on the way to becoming a sloppy drunk like my uncle Jim. So I didn't feel very sorry about that."

"You must have been a levelheaded young woman."

"I don't think anyone ever accused me of that."

"Think about the beer. You said it tasted bitter. But you drank it anyway?"

"A couple of sips. Three, maybe. I was mostly interested in what Alice was doing."

"Which was what?"

"She was looking out the window beside our table.

Just drinking her pretty little cocktail and watching the alley behind the bar."

"What was she watching for?"

"I wasn't sure. And when I asked, she told me she was just bored." Charlie frowned, realizing the strangeness of what she'd just said. "On our big, transgressive night out. That's strange, isn't it?"

"I don't know. I didn't know Alice."

"It *was* strange. The whole night was strange. And then, suddenly, Alice grabbed my arm and said it was time to go."

"Go where?" Lauren asked.

Charlie got up and started walking, her steps a little unsteady. She could feel Alice's hand curled around her wrist, tugging her along as they left the bar and stepped out into the chilly winter night.

Only, she wasn't walking, was she? Not really. She was still seated on the sofa in Mike's living room. Lauren Pell sat in one of the armchairs across the coffee table from her, and Mike was a big warm presence somewhere to her right. But the cold breeze sent a chill skittering through her, and the scent of Alice's favorite perfume wafted toward her as they entered the alley behind the Headhunter Bar.

There's someone out here, Charlie thought. She could hear voices, shaping words that she couldn't quite make out. A man's voice. Maybe a woman's. Charlie couldn't tell for sure.

And it was dark. So dark. The only light came from the dim illumination through the tinted windows inside the bar and one faint light burning inside the cinder block building across the alley from the bar.

There was someone inside the building. Charlie could make out moving shadows through the thin curtains in the building's windows.

But the world was starting to twirl around her. Twirl and twist, growing incrementally darker.

She felt herself falling. Arms wrapped around her, and Alice's perfume filled her lungs. Suddenly, she was on the ground, her face pressed against the damp pavement where the alley intersected with the side street.

"I'm sorry, Charlie," Alice said quietly, her voice almost mournful, "but I have to do the rest of this by myself."

The world seemed so dark. For a long time, there was a universe of nothingness so dense, so vast, that it terrified her. Her breath came in hard gasps as the panic rose inside her, hot and bitter like bile. "The world has disappeared!" she gasped.

"You're okay, Charlie." Lauren's voice was low and soothing. "You can go to your safe place if you need to."

Charlie pictured herself in Mike's arms. Felt them around her, solid and warm. It wasn't the safe place she had originally considered when Lauren had walked her through how they were going to approach the hypnosis session, but it felt right.

Mike was her safe place.

Her breathing settled into a regular cadence, and the panic subsided.

"Do you want to keep going?" Lauren asked.

"Yes."

"You were unconscious, weren't you?"

"I must have been. I think Alice drugged my beer." Charlie frowned. "She was planning something. I knew she was. And it had something to do with that building across the alley from the bar."

"You don't know what that building was?"

She thought about it, tried to picture the place. "The alley was behind it. I'm not sure I even know what street the building must have faced. I didn't spend a lot of time in Mercerville when I was younger. It was sort of the big city to me then." She laughed at the thought. "Little Mercerville as the big city. Isn't that something?"

"Let's not worry too much about that building. That's information we can track down later," Lauren said. "I'm more interested in what happened when the world came back to you."

Tension built low in her spine. "I don't remember."

"Are you sure? Maybe you just don't want to remember."

Charlie shook her head. "I do want to. It's just a blank."

"You told me before we started that you had a memory of seeing Alice dead. Can you recall that moment?"

Charlie shivered, but she let her mind return to the dark alley. She was past the gravel, lying facedown on the pavement at the edge of the road. Peavine Road, she remembered. That was where Alice's body had been found.

She opened her eyes, bracing herself for what she knew she'd see.

But Alice wasn't dead.

She stood in the middle of Peavine Road, crying. Her blouse had been torn at the shoulder, and her wavy blond hair was tousled and frizzy from the light drizzle falling. The light on the corner seemed to glow underwater as fog rolled into the streets, washing everything in a dreamy haze.

Charlie tried to call Alice's name, but her tongue was thick. And Alice wasn't listening to anyone. Not even the man who stood nearby, talking to her in fast, tense tones.

When it happened, it was fast and shocking. A large black sedan, moving fast and strangely quiet, the motor hum barely audible over the thudding bass beat coming from inside the nearby bar. It slammed into Alice from behind, hitting her waist high and sending her flying up into the air. She landed on the trunk of the moving car and rolled off, slamming into the pavement with a sickening thud.

"I saw it happen," Charlie rasped, her heart racing with shock. "I saw Alice killed."

"Can you remember anything about the car?"

"It was big and black. A sedan. It looked expensive, but I'm not an expert on cars. I remember the engine was quiet. I think that's why it seems like an expensive car to me. No rattling engine or faulty muffler."

"You said you heard a man's voice talking to Alice. What do you remember about it?"

"It seemed familiar. It still does, but I can't place it."

"You're lying on the side of the road still. You're seeing Alice's body in the road. You must be feeling shocked and traumatized."

Cold crept into her skin. "Yes. I feel as if it's not real, even though I just saw it happen. I think I need to get to Alice, I need to help her. But I can't move. I can only watch the blood spreading across the pavement beneath her head."

"What about the man who was talking to Alice? Can you tell what he's doing?"

"He's walking into the road. I can't see anything but his back."

"What is he wearing?"

"Jeans. A jacket—maybe a rain jacket. It has a hood." Her breath caught. "Like the man I saw in the alley last night."

She watched the man bend close to Alice's body. He reached out one shaking hand as if to touch her, but he pulled it back at the last minute.

But not before his sleeve pulled away from his arm, revealing a half-moon scar on the inside of his wrist. "Oh, my God. He has a scar on his wrist. A half-moon scar."

On instinct, she reached out for Mike. He caught her hand, and the cold, dark alley disappeared. She was in Mike's living room again, seated near a warm fire. Lauren Pell sat across from her, her expression curious.

"I know who the man was," Charlie said. "I remember. He stood up and turned toward me. I saw his face." Even now, the features of the man's face were so clear in her mind, she wondered why she'd never been able to recall them before now. Sandy hair, wisps peeking out from the rain jacket's hood. Cool blue eyes, dark with fear. Straight, sharp features twisted with shock and desperation.

"Who was it?" Mike asked.

"Randall Feeney. Craig Bearden's chief aide."

"ARE YOU SURE he wasn't the person in the car?" Archer Trask asked Charlie. He and Maddox Heller had returned to Mike's house at Mike's request shortly after Lauren Pell departed. She'd left a recording of the hypnosis session with Mike and Charlie, which they'd played for the two men soon after they arrived.

"Pretty sure. I heard him talking to Alice right before she was hit." Sitting next to Mike, Charlie seemed to have recovered from the hypnosis session for the most part, though there was a strained sadness in her hazel eyes that made Mike's heart hurt.

Witnessing the murder of her best friend had clearly traumatized her so much that she'd repressed those memories. She still believed she'd been drugged, but some of the memories she'd thought were gone had, instead, been concealed beneath the trauma.

"But he saw the hit-and-run and never told anyone," Mike added. "So we think he must have some idea who was driving."

"When we went out into the alley, I heard voices.

I couldn't make them out. I can't say for sure if they were male or female. But I think they were in that building behind the bar."

"That was the Mercerville branch of Craig Bearden's campaign for state senator," Trask said. "I remember because when we canvassed the area for potential witnesses, it was one of the places we stopped. I remember wondering if Bearden would ever step foot in the place again, knowing his daughter died in the street just a few yards away."

"Did he?" Mike asked, curious.

"Never did. They closed the office and sold the property. Took the proceeds and started a scholarship fund in Alice's name."

"Feeney was never questioned?"

"No. He didn't have any motive, as far as anyone knew. Bearden and his wife both said Alice preferred to stay out of her father's political campaign, so she didn't have much contact with anyone in his office. And we started focusing on the idea that she'd been hit by a driver under the influence, considering how close it had been to the bar."

"But we have a problem going after Feeney, don't we?" Heller said.

"We do," Trask admitted, looking at Charlie. "No offense, but your memories aren't going to give us any kind of legal probable cause to bring him in for questioning. He'll lawyer up and we won't have a leg to stand on."

Charlie looked at Mike, frustration shining in her eyes. He reached over and caught her hand, giving it an encouraging squeeze. She squeezed back and lifted her chin, turning her gaze back to Trask. "So, let's figure out a way to come up with a little probable cause."

Something in the tone of Charlie's voice sent a ripple of tension through Mike's gut. Across from them, Archer Trask frowned, his eyes narrowing.

"Just what do you have in mind?" he asked Charlie.

"If we're right, Feeney intercepted the phone call I made to Craig Bearden, telling him I was starting to remember more about the night Alice died. And after that, he started following me and then tampered with my brakes and broke into my house to scare me off. Maybe twice, if Mike is right about the scar he saw on the intruder's wrist. Then, last night, he apparently drugged Mike so he'd have a clear path to me. I think he was planning to kill me."

"I think you're probably right," Trask agreed.

"So maybe we should offer him what he wants."

"Charlie—" Mike began warningly.

"I think we should set a trap for Randall Feeney. With me as the bait."

Chapter Sixteen

"This is a crazy idea." Mike stopped in the middle of his restless pacing to face Charlie. "You don't need to be there." Ever since Charlie had proposed her plan earlier, all Mike could do was try to come up with reasons why it was a terrible idea.

"Yes. I do. He's tracking us somehow. He needs to see you drop me off at my house alone or he's not going to make his move."

"Oh. I forgot to tell you. We think we know how he's following us." Mike told her about the tracker attached to his truck. "Heller said he left it there, so Feeney knows we're still here."

"He's still going to assume you'll be with me."

Mike started pacing again. "I just don't think you need to put your head in the noose to make this work."

"Well, I do. And Trask and Heller both agree."

Mike grimaced. "They're thinking of the case. Not you."

Charlie crossed until she blocked his path. "I *am* the case."

"Not to me." He cupped her face between his large

hands, his touch so gentle it made her chest ache. "You're not just a case to me."

She laid her hands over his. "I know. And you're not just a bodyguard to me, either."

He bent and kissed her forehead, then pulled her into his arms, pressing his face into her hair. When he spoke, his breath was warm against her cheek. "I want this done. I want you to be free and safe. I need that."

She stroked his broad, strong back, marveling at the solid feel of him beneath her fingers. He was a man of steel, inside and out, strong in all the ways she admired.

And he admired her, too. That was the crazy, intoxicating part of their burgeoning relationship. He wanted her, yes. That was evident in the fiery desire she saw in his eyes sometimes when he looked at her. But he also liked her. Respected her choices, even when, like now, they drove him crazy.

She wasn't used to being admired and respected by anyone.

"I can do this," she said, pulling her head back to look into his worried green eyes. "It'll be okay."

"I hope so." He caressed her cheek. "But does it have to be tonight? Can't we have just one more night to ourselves?"

"Just one?"

His eyes narrowed, and he kissed her. Hard and deep, a kiss that sent her head swirling and her heart racing. And he pulled away all too soon, crossing to stand by the fireplace, his gaze directed toward the flickering flames. "Never just one," he growled.

"After tonight, we can have as many nights as we want."

He gave her a look so full of promise she thought her heart would burst, but before she could take a step toward him, the perimeter alarm went off, and Mike instantly went on full alert.

He had added a front door camera connected to a phone app after his mother's unexpected arrival had caught them off guard. He checked his phone and relaxed marginally. "The cavalry," he murmured as he went to the door to greet the new arrivals.

Besides Heller and Trask, a slim redhead about Charlie's size entered, flashing a brief smile at Mike before she turned her attention to Charlie. "Not a perfect match," she murmured. "But it'll work from a distance."

"What's going on?" Charlie asked.

"Mike's right. There's no need to put you in needless danger. This is Meredith Chandler. She works at the agency. Meredith, this is Charlie Winters. And you know Mike."

Charlie looked at Meredith, taking in the short red hair, tall, slim build and pale complexion. They resembled in general, though no one would mistake them up close. Partly because Meredith was drop-dead gorgeous and partly because she walked with the grace of a dancer instead of Charlie's ungainly gait.

But all Meredith would have to do, Charlie presumed, was walk up the flagstone path from the driveway to the front door of Charlie's house and go inside. Feeney would be trying to stay out of sight, which would make it hard to tell one tall, slim redhead from another.

"He's not going to buy that you'd just drop me off at my house by myself," Charlie said to Mike.

"We agree," Trask said, "but we have an idea."

By the time he finished telling Charlie and Mike what they had planned, even Mike agreed it was a pretty good idea.

"I checked with Bill Hardy. He's got your brakes repaired, so your car is ready to go. Mike will drive Meredith there to pick it up. We've warned Bill that someone besides you will be picking it up. Mike will pay. Meredith will drive the car home with Mike bringing up the rear."

"Halfway there, my truck suddenly develops problems and I have to pull over to see what's wrong, while Meredith drives on." Mike nodded slowly. "If Feeney's following us, that'll give him time to catch her alone."

"Only, she won't be alone. We'll be there," Heller said.

"What if he runs the minute he sees Meredith isn't me?"

"I don't think he's going to confront you. He'll sneak, like he's been sneaking this whole time. He may try to break in and catch you unaware. Either way, we'll be there and we'll be ready," Trask assured her.

"I'll get a signal from Heller once things start to go down," Mike said, "and I'll get to the house for backup. Meanwhile, you'll be here behind locked doors, with a perimeter alarm to let you know if there's an intruder. I put the app on your phone, too, so all you have to do is check it and you'll be able to see whoever's approaching. If you feel threatened at all, I'm a phone call away."

"It sounds…very planned out," Charlie said.

Mike crossed to her side and took her hands in his. "You can say no to all of this if you want."

Charlie shook her head. "Why would I say no? I'm the only one who won't be in danger."

Mike squeezed her hands. "I know you don't like sitting on the sidelines, but—"

"I don't like sitting on the sidelines?" She quirked an eyebrow. "I'm a sideline-sitter from way back, Mike. I'm a pro at it."

"I know better," he said softly. "But this time, I need you to be safe, okay? I need you right here where you can't get hurt."

She wanted to argue, not liking the idea of a stranger she'd just met moments earlier putting her neck on the line so Charlie could be safe. But Meredith Chandler had assured her that she was well trained. Former FBI agent, plus fresh off the new-hire training program Campbell Cove Security had mandated company wide. She would be an asset to the mission.

Charlie would just be in the way.

"Okay," she said finally. "Let's do it. I'll make the call to the campaign office, ask Mr. Bearden to meet me at my house in an hour, and if it goes like we think it will, we can get this show on the road."

What she hadn't anticipated, however, was Randall

Feeney answering the phone at the campaign office himself. Charlie's throat closed up for a moment, and he said "Hello?" a second time.

She cleared her throat. "This is Charlie Winters. Is Mr. Bearden in?"

This time, it was Feeney who didn't speak. Finally, he asked, "He's not here this afternoon. May I take a message?"

"I was hoping to talk with him personally. In fact, I really need to see him in person." She glanced at the others, who stood nearby, waiting for word to move.

"I'm not sure what his calendar is like today," Feeney said hesitantly.

"Please try to contact him. It's urgent. I need to talk to him about what happened to Alice. I've remembered more information and I wanted to get his opinion about the things that are coming back to me. I'll be at my house in about an hour, and I should be there for the rest of the afternoon. My address is 425 Sycamore Street in Campbell Cove. Please let him know. It's important."

"I'll see if I can reach him."

"Thank you." Charlie hung up the phone, her hands shaking. "It was Feeney himself."

"Perfect," Trask said.

"If we're right about who attached that tracker to Mike's truck, that's how he'll be following you. He'll be looking for a way to separate you from Mike." Heller picked up the small gym bag he'd brought with him and put it on the coffee table. Unzipped, the bag revealed its contents—four small earpieces. Heller handed them out. "We can communicate through these, in case anything starts to go wrong."

"Don't I get one of those?" Charlie asked.

The other four looked at her blankly.

"Oh, okay. I just sit here and worry. Got it."

Mike crossed to her side. "It'll be over before you know it. I'll be back here, Feeney will be in custody and we'll be on our way to finding out who was behind the wheel of that car."

She sighed, knowing he was right. The wait for word would be interminable, but she'd be a hell of a lot safer here than she would be out there with Mike and the others.

That was the important point, wasn't it?

Trask and Heller left together soon afterward, wanting to be out of sight in case Feeney did a drive-by to see if Mike and Charlie were leaving together. Meredith went to the guest bedroom to find some of Charlie's clothes to wear, leaving Mike and Charlie alone in the living room.

He crossed to where she stood by the fireplace, wrapping his arms around her from behind. "This is going to work."

"You're right," she said, although tension thrummed deep in her chest.

"I'll be back before you miss me."

"Not possible." She turned in his arms to look at him. "You come back to me all in one piece. Understand? This is nonnegotiable."

"Yes, ma'am."

She caught his face between her palms, enjoying

the light rasp of his beard stubble against her skin. "Taking your self-defense course was the best decision I ever made in my whole crazy life."

He smiled at her. "I knew the minute you walked into my class that first morning you would be nothing but trouble." He kissed her nose. "And you are. But I have a real soft spot for trouble."

The sound of a clearing throat nearby made him groan, and Charlie pulled out of his arms and turned to face Meredith. She'd donned a pair of Charlie's jeans and a bright green T-shirt that was one of her favorites. Her red hair peeked out from beneath a blue University of Kentucky baseball cap. "Think I'll pass as Charlie?"

"Close enough," Mike said. "You ready to go?"

"Yeah."

Mike turned back to Charlie. "Watch TV. Or read. Just try not to worry. We know what we're doing." He gave her a quick kiss and nodded for Meredith to follow him as he headed for the door to the garage.

Watch TV, Charlie thought. *Read a book. Try not to worry.*

As if she'd be able to do any of those things.

THE FIRST PART of the plan went through without a hitch. Meredith used Charlie's credit card to pay for the repairs, and Bill Hardy, forewarned, put the transaction through without question. He handed over the keys to Charlie's Toyota and waved them off.

Back in the Ford by himself, Mike called in his position. In the Toyota, Meredith did the same.

"Feeney's on the move," Trask said on his end. He and Heller were positioned inside Charlie's house, hidden in case Feeney decided to stage some sort of ambush.

"How do we know?" Mike asked.

"I put one of my deputies on his tail."

"You might have mentioned that before," Mike muttered. "What if he spots the tail?"

"He won't." Trask sounded confident.

Mike was coming up on the intersection of Mill Road and Old Mercerville Highway. As good a place to have a breakdown as any.

Ahead, the Toyota crossed the intersection. But Mike pulled over to the side of the road and parked on the shoulder, turning on his emergency flashers. He waited for a couple of cars to pass, then got out of the truck and walked around to the hood.

He lifted the hood and pulled up the rod to hold it in place. "I'm stopped at Mill Road and Old Mercerville Highway," he murmured into the small mike that protruded from the earpiece. To anyone looking, it would seem as if he was on the phone using a Bluetooth headset.

"Feeney is driving a silver Honda Accord. He looks to be headed directly your way."

While pretending to be checking the water in the radiator, Mike kept one eye on the light traffic passing by him. Sure enough, one of the next cars to pass was a silver Honda. He could barely make out a male driver, who seemed to be the only person in the vehicle.

"I have a visual. Subject is heading down Mill Road. Should be nearing Sycamore Road in two minutes."

"I'm about three minutes ahead," Meredith said. "I'm about to turn into the driveway at Charlie's place."

"Showtime," Trask said. "You know what to do, Strong."

Mike fiddled with the radiator for a few seconds more, until he was sure Feeney's Honda was well out of sight. He double-checked with a glance over his shoulder, then closed the truck's hood and returned to the driver's seat. He turned off the hazard lights, started the truck and pulled back onto the road.

CHARLIE CHECKED THE clock over the fireplace mantel for about the twentieth time in the past half hour. By now, Meredith would be at the house. Trask and Heller would have arrived there a few minutes earlier, setting up for the ambush.

All she had to do was wait and it would all be over.

The trill of her cell phone made her jump. She picked it up off the coffee table and checked the display.

A familiar number jumped out at her. Her heart started to thud faster in her chest.

"Hello?"

"Charlotte. It's been a long time." Diana Bearden's voice hadn't changed in ten years. Still soft and warm. Tinged with a hint of wary friendliness.

"Mrs. Bearden. I...wasn't expecting to hear from you."

"I know. I'm sorry about the distance over these years. I just— It's been hard to be reminded of Alice's death."

"It's been hard for me, too." Charlie blinked back the tears suddenly burning her eyes. "I thought about trying to contact you and Mr. Bearden about a thousand times. I did call Mr. Bearden's office a few weeks back. And today." She paused, remembering the reason for her latest call.

"Craig's out of town. He's in Louisville for a meet and greet. I was going to go, but..." Her voice trailed off, and for a moment, Charlie thought she'd hung up.

"Mrs. Bearden?"

There were tears in her voice when she spoke again. "I'm sorry, Charlotte. It's just so near the time...you know. And hearing your voice again after so long brings up so many memories."

"I'm sorry." Tears pricked Charlie's eyes.

"I don't suppose you have a few minutes to meet with me today, do you?" Diana asked. "Maybe you could come by the house?"

"I—I don't have my car."

"Then maybe I could come to you?"

"No. That's not good, either." She thought about Mike and the others, probably neck-deep in danger as they spoke. He'd told her to stay put. Her safety was on the line.

"I just— I'm feeling so alone right now. Craig doesn't understand. He's poured all his grief into his campaign. It's like he thinks he can make everything right by winning and changing laws that might have saved Alice all those years ago. But it won't bring her back." Diana was crying helplessly now. "Nothing will ever bring her back. And I just— I need to talk to someone who understands. I think you understand, don't you, Charlotte?"

Charlie bit back a sob. "Okay. You can come here." She gave Diana the address. "I'll be waiting."

"Thank you," Diana said quietly. "You just may be saving my life. I'll be there in a few minutes." She hung up the phone.

Charlie put her phone back on the coffee table and sat on the sofa, gripping her hands tightly together. Now that she'd agreed to see Diana, she was already second-guessing her decision. Mike would probably be furious at her for agreeing to have Diana Bearden come here. And maybe it had been a stupid decision.

But how could she say no to Alice's mother after all this time?

She checked her phone, in case Mike had left a message while she was talking to Diana. But her voice mail was empty.

The clock over the mantel showed only seven minutes had passed since the last time she checked.

What was happening at her house now?

"FEENEY'S PARKED HIS CAR. The GPS signal hasn't moved for two minutes." Trask's voice sounded tinny through the earpiece.

"Do you have a location?" Mike asked.

"Somewhere between here and Mill Road. What's your position?"

"I've just pulled onto Sycamore. I'll keep an eye out for the Honda."

He spotted the vehicle about two blocks farther down Sycamore Road, parked at the curb about a half mile from Charlie's house.

"Found it," he said into the mike. "Half mile up Sycamore. Unoccupied. Feeney must be on foot."

He pulled the truck up behind the Honda and got out, reaching down to unsheathe his boot knife as he walked. He looked into the car's interior to be sure Feeney wasn't hiding, then he shoved the blade of the knife into the front and back tires on the street-facing side of the Honda.

"Vehicle's incapacitated," he said into the mike. "Got a visual on Feeney yet?"

"Nothing yet." It was Heller who answered. "Be careful. Don't want him to spot you."

"Got it covered." Mike cut through a side yard and headed into the thick woods that stood behind the homes on this part of Sycamore Road. Once hidden within the trees, he pulled the pot of camouflage paint from his backpack and covered his face to match the camo jacket and pants he wore.

The afternoon had waned quickly since Charlie had made the call, twilight already drifting over the afternoon on gathering dark clouds, bringing with them the threat of rain. It also provided better cover for Mike as he tried to make up the time he'd already lost, but it also made him a little wary about Charlie stuck at his house alone with darkness falling.

"We have a visual." Trask's voice buzzed in his ear as he crept through the trees behind the house next door to Charlie's. He paused in place, peering through the thicket in hopes of catching sight of Randall Feeney.

There. He was dressed in dark colors, moving through the woods about forty yards east of Mike's position.

"Showtime," he whispered.

Chapter Seventeen

The wind picked up, swirling dead leaves around
Mike's feet as he crept closer to where Randall Feeney crouched near the edge of the woods directly behind Charlie's house. For one heart-stopping moment,
Feeney turned his head toward Mike, who froze in
place, holding his breath.

Then, as rain started to fall in fat drops from the
gunmetal sky, Feeney dashed through the backyard
and up to the side of the house. He looked around him,
checking for any sign that he was being watched, then
he pulled open a small window built into the house's
foundation.

It was a tiny space, but Feeney was a slim man.
He squeezed through the opening and slipped inside.

Mike muttered a curse. He should have checked
the house for just that sort of point of entry. He'd
made sure that all the windows on the upper floor
were locked, but he hadn't even thought about there
being a cellar in the small house. He should have
asked Charlie.

He should have done a lot of things differently.

"Feeney's entered through a cellar window. I didn't even think to check if it was locked. He'll probably be coming up through an interior door." Mike followed Feeney's path to the window and crouched to one side, listening through the opening for any sounds the man might be making.

Taking a chance, he peered through the narrow window into the cellar. The small, musty space was utterly dark, the gloom alleviated only by the faint gray light from the window and the narrow beam of a small flashlight several yards inside the space.

Feeney was crouching near the back of the cellar, next to what looked like a furnace unit. His body blocked whatever it was he was doing, but based on where he was crouching, he seemed to be near the pipes.

What was he doing?

Suddenly, Feeney stood and started to turn back to the window.

Mike pulled back quickly, heart racing, and flattened himself against the wall.

Something came flying out of the window and hit the ground, sliding across the wet grass. It looked like a coil of green twine.

But it wasn't. And suddenly, Mike knew exactly what Randall Feeney had been doing in the cellar.

He scrambled toward the green coil, growling into the headset's mouthpiece, "He's cut the gas line in the furnace room beneath the house. He's going to try to blow it up. Get the hell out now!"

Several things happened at once. Feeney's head

and shoulders appeared in the window as he started to haul himself out. Mike grabbed the green coil of cannon fuse and pulled out his knife, slicing the leading piece of fuse trailing from the window. He flung the coil toward the tree line with one hand and leveled the knife toward Feeney, who had stopped half in and half out of the house.

"Very careful, Mr. Feeney," he warned as the man stared back at him with wide, scared eyes. "You've just armed a very nasty bomb, and I wouldn't want to see you blown up with it."

Heller came around the side of the house, half-crouched, ready to spring. "Trask just turned off the master gas switch. If nobody does anything stupid, we can end this thing with everybody still alive."

Trask appeared then, Meredith Chandler right behind him. He eased over to the basement window and nodded for Heller to join him. The two men pulled Feeney out of the window and jerked him to his feet.

"I want a lawyer," Feeney said.

"That can be arranged," Trask said, pushing Feeney toward the wall of the house. "Spread your legs and put your hands against the wall."

Feeney complied.

"Anything in your pockets I need to know about? Needles, weapons?"

"A lighter in my front pocket. A phone in the back."

Trask pulled the lighter and the phone from Feeney's pockets and handed them to Mike to hold while he patted his prisoner down.

The phone vibrated suddenly against Mike's palm. He looked at the display and saw a message from someone called D. The girl isn't there. I'll take it from here.

His heart plummeting, he crossed to Feeney and shoved the phone in front of his face. "Who is D?"

Feeney just looked at him, a faint smile curving his lips.

Mike showed Trask the message. "We knew he probably had an accomplice, whoever was driving the car that hit Alice."

Mike sent a text back. Where are you now?

There was no response.

"Damn it, Feeney, who is D?"

Feeney continued smiling.

THE PERIMETER ALARM sounded in the hallway just as Charlie was finishing a quick application of lipstick. It was silly, she knew, to worry about how she looked after all these years, but maybe that was why it seemed so important to her. It was her first face-to-face meeting with Alice's mother in almost ten years. She wanted to show a little respect for the occasion.

She was halfway to the door when she remembered the camera app on her phone. Pulling it up, she checked the camera feed.

Diana Bearden stood in front of the door, her image slightly distorted by the camera lens. Charlie knew from her press photos that she hadn't aged much in the past ten years, but she was struck anew by how much Diana looked like her daughter might have looked if she had grown into middle age.

Giving her hair a quick finger combing, she shoved her phone in the pocket of her jeans and unlocked the door.

For a moment, Diana just stared back at her through the screen door, her blue eyes sharp and probing, as if she were trying to read past Charlie's exterior to see what existed at the core of her soul. It was a disconcerting sensation, forcing Charlie to paste on a smile and open the screen door. "I'm so glad you're here," she said as she stepped back to let Diana inside.

After locking the door behind them, she turned around to look at Alice's mother, mentally rehearsing what she wanted to say. *I'm sorry* came to mind, along with *I miss Alice like crazy.*

She was so caught up in what she thought she should say that it took a couple of seconds to register what she was seeing in front of her.

Diana held a pistol in one perfectly manicured hand, the barrel pointed straight at Charlie's heart.

"You just couldn't let it go, could you?" Diana said.

Her heart sinking, Charlie slowly shook her head. "No. I couldn't."

A VIBRATION AGAINST his hip drew Mike's attention briefly away from Randall Feeney's smiling face. It was his phone, sending him a notice that the perimeter alarm at his house had been breached.

"Someone's breached the perimeter at my house," he told Heller, already moving toward the front of the house. He pulled up the camera app and checked the feed, stumbling to a halt in surprise as he recognized the tawny-haired woman in a dark blue suit who stood at his door.

What was Diana Bearden doing at his house?

He punched in Charlie's cell phone number. The call went directly to voice mail.

Heller had caught up, grabbing Mike by the shoulder. "What the hell is going on?"

"Diana Bearden is at my house. Charlie just let her in." The tail end of the motion-activated camera shot showed Charlie letting Diana inside. The door closed, and a few seconds later, the shot went dormant.

"Diana," Heller said, his voice dropping in pitch.

D, Mike thought, his heart suddenly stuttering. He turned to look at Heller. "It was Diana Bearden. She was Feeney's accomplice."

"And now she's at your house with Charlie."

Mike started running before Heller finished his sentence.

"I don't remember everything, you know." Charlie tried to control the tremors running through her as she stared down the barrel of Diana's pistol. It couldn't be very large, she realized—it fit rather snugly in Diana's small hand. But the big black hole at the end of the barrel still appeared to be enormous, and it never wavered from the center of her chest.

Center mass, she thought. Wasn't that what shooting instructors called it? The center of the body, where most of the body's vital organs lay. One or two shots there, and nobody would be walking away.

"You remember enough," Diana said. "That's why you called my husband again today, isn't it?"

"Feeney told you?"

"He tells me everything." Diana twitched the barrel of the pistol toward the center of the living room. "Where's the bathroom?"

The question caught Charlie off guard. "You want to go to the bathroom? Now?"

Diana laughed. "No, I want you to go there. Now."

Charlie walked slowly down the hallway toward the bathroom door on the right. As they passed the open door of the office, she spotted His Highness sitting in the doorway, his blue eyes glaring hate at Diana Bearden. He bared his teeth and hissed.

Diana swung the pistol toward the cat. Hizzy stood his ground, growling.

It was the distraction Charlie needed. She pitched her shoulder into Diana's chest, slamming hard against her sternum. A grunt of pain erupted from the woman's throat, and she tumbled into the wall, her head cracking against the door frame.

As her gun hand hit the ground, Charlie stomped on her wrist with her full weight, feeling the bones beneath her feet crack. The gun fell loose from Diana's fingers as she howled in pain. Charlie kicked it away and straddled Diana's waist, pinning her to the floor with both hands.

"You were in the car!" she cried, adrenaline pumping through her like venom. "You hit Alice with your car, on purpose! You let her die. You let me think it was all my fault! How could you do that to your daughter?"

Diana tried to fight free of Charlie's grasp, but her broken wrist was useless, and Charlie was bigger and stronger, now that there wasn't a pistol to equalize things between them.

"Why?" Charlie wailed, tears burning a path down her cheeks. "Why did you do that to Alice?"

"Because she knew!" Diana screamed. "She knew and she was going to tell Craig what we were doing."

The light in the cinder block building behind the Headhunter Bar, Charlie realized. The voices she'd heard when she entered the alley had been coming from there. From the old Bearden campaign head-quarters.

"Alice was looking for you that night. That's why she'd talked me into going to that bar. She knew it was the best place to watch the old campaign office. Because she knew you were meeting someone there when Mr. Bearden was out of town. Didn't she?"

Diana just stared at her a moment, then bucked her hips, trying to knock Charlie off her.

Charlie pressed hard on Diana's broken wrist, and she screamed.

"You were afraid she'd tell Craig. It would ruin everything. Craig's political career would fall apart. Your dreams of being a senator's wife would be down the toilet. And Feeney would lose his cushy little job as a toady if Craig knew. You couldn't let that happen.

Alice—" Her voice faltered, but she gritted her teeth and forced the words out of her aching throat. "Your daughter, your only child, was acceptable collateral damage. Was that it?"

The sound of a key in the lock drew her attention away from Diana's baleful glare. The older woman made one last attempt at escape, shoving the heel of her hand into Charlie's chin, snapping her head back.

Charlie's grip on Diana faltered, and Diana shoved her off, sending her reeling into the wall. Charlie scrambled after the other woman as she bolted for the end of the hall, where the gun had landed in the middle of the kitchen floor.

She tackled Diana by the legs and scrambled forward over her back, jerking Diana's left hand away as her fingers brushed against the butt of the pistol.

She heard heavy footfalls coming up behind her. "I've got her, Charlie." Mike's voice, low and reassuring, sent a little shudder darting down her spine.

She leaned forward and shoved the gun sideways. It skittered farther into the kitchen, landing under the kitchen table. Then she scrambled forward, off Diana, and turned to look at Mike.

He spared her a quick, intense look that made her stomach turn inside out before he holstered his gun, reached down and hauled Diana Bearden to her feet.

Maddox Heller entered the hall behind Mike and Diana, pistol in hand. He skidded to a stop, taking in the whole tableau. His shoulders relaxed, and he dropped the pistol to his side. "You good here?"

"We're good," Mike said, his gaze locking with Charlie's again. "And you can take Charlie off my self-defense course roster when you get back to the academy."

Heller put his pistol back in the holster under his jacket. "Yeah? Why's that?"

Mike shot Charlie a lopsided grin. "Because she already passed."

"FEENEY PUT MOST of it on Diana Bearden," Trask told Mike and Charlie a few hours later. "But we caught him red-handed trying to blow up Charlie's house, so he's not getting away with anything."

"Did he admit to drugging Mike?" Charlie asked.

"He said Diana blackmailed him into it. Apparently he's been skimming money from Bearden's campaign coffers, and he thought Diana was covering it up for him. But apparently she was smart enough to make sure all the stink would fall on him once it came to light."

"Do you believe him?" Mike asked.

"Yeah, I think he's realized the truth is about the only defense he has."

"Did he say why he drugged me? What was he going to do?" Mike asked.

Trask glanced at Charlie. "I think we both know what he was going to do."

Next to Mike, Charlie shivered. He put his arm around her, pulling her closer.

"How did Diana know Charlie was at my house? She'd already sent Feeney to blow up her house."

"She's not talking, but Feeney told us Diana was beginning to suspect we were onto Feeney. So we think when Charlie called out of the blue and left that message about remembering things, Diana thought it might be a setup." Trask's smile looked like a grimace. "She called you, learned quickly that you weren't where you were supposed to be and figured out you were alone."

"So she made her move." Charlie sighed. "I used to wish my mother was just like Mrs. Bearden."

Mike tightened his arm around her. "I'm glad she's not."

Charlie looked up at Archer Trask. "Are we done here?"

"For now. We'll probably have more questions soon, but I think we're good for today."

Outside, a cold, misty rain had begun to fall. Mike hurried Charlie to his truck and helped her into the passenger seat. Once he took his place behind the wheel, he turned the heat up. "Better?"

She flashed him a sheepish smile. "I'm not that cold, but I can't seem to stop shaking."

"That's delayed reaction. But I have a prescription for that." He shot her a quick smile.

"Oh?" She turned to look at him. "What's that, Dr. Strong?"

"Well, it starts with a big cup of hot chocolate with whipped cream. Then there's a roaring fire and a blanket big enough for two—"

"I'm sold," she said with a big grin that made his insides sizzle. "How fast can we get there?"

By THE TIME the local news moved on to another story besides the scandalous tale of adultery, betrayal and murder among the rich and famous, a week had passed. Hizzy's stitches had been removed and the cone of shame relegated to the trash bin, Charlie's insurance money had paid for new furniture and a state-of-the-art security system, and Mike's mother had reluctantly returned home to Black Rock, North Carolina, with a promise from Mike and Charlie to visit for Christmas.

Mike finished pushing Charlie's sofa into place near the fireplace and dusted his hands on his jeans. "Happy now?"

She walked over to where he stood near the hearth, wrapping her arms around his waist. "Delirious."

He grinned down at her, enfolding her in a tight embrace. "Good. I intend to keep you that way. Delirious Charlie is my favorite flavor." He bent to kiss her, his tongue sliding over her lips as if sampling her taste. "Yup, definitely my favorite."

"Let's not get ahead of ourselves," she warned, gently extricating herself from his embrace. "We have one more thing to add before the room will be complete."

Mike groaned. "Don't tell me you bought a second sofa."

She gave his arm a light tug. "No, just something that would make that corner look absolutely perfect." She led him into the mudroom, where she'd stashed her newest purchase.

Mike stared at the little fir tree leaning against the window in the small room. "A tree."

"A *Christmas* tree," she corrected, picking up the new plastic bin she'd bought earlier that day for all the ornaments she'd purchased during her buying spree. She carried the box into the living room, leaving Mike to haul the tree and its stand.

Together, they set up the tree in the corner and arranged the red velvet tree skirt at the bottom. "It already looks lovely," she said with a happy sigh.

"So, a Christmas fan," Mike said, smiling at her. "I'll add that to my list of important things to know about Charlie."

Unexpected tears pricked her eyes. She blinked them back as she opened the plastic bin and pulled out a new packet of silver garland. "I wasn't, you know. Not for a long time." She ran the strands of silver tinsel through her fingers. "Not after Alice died. It was so close to Christmas, I could never seem to muster up the mood."

Mike took the garland from her hands and pulled her into his arms. "I'm sorry. I know this can't be easy for you, especially now."

She leaned her head against his chest, taking comfort from the strong, steady beat of his heart beneath her ear. She thought about the pages she'd written about Alice, about her own memories of that night. She had hoped by writing everything down, she could make sense of what had happened.

But there was no sense in what happened. Only sadness and bittersweet release. It was time to close that file and write something new. Something brighter. Something full of hope and meaning.

"I know now," she said. "I know what happened to her and why. It makes me so sad for her. And grateful that she never knew how her mother betrayed her. But knowing means I can finally let it go. Alice wouldn't have wanted me to mourn her forever."

"No, from the way you've described her, I don't think she'd have been happy about that at all."

She drew her head back to look at him. "She'd have liked you. Big, strong, badass. She might have fought me for you. Might have even won."

He bent his head and kissed her nose. "Not a chance, Charlie. Not a chance in this world."

"Are we finally having that talk about us we kept threatening to have?" she asked, cuddling closer.

"I guess we are. So I'll go first. I'm all in, Charlie. You're it for me. I think I knew it from the first time you stepped into my class that day, all spitfire and trouble."

She grinned. "You make me sound so interesting."

"You are. The most interesting woman I've ever known."

"And that," she said with a light pat on his backside, "is why you're it for me, Mike Strong. Because you're apparently blind and a little on the dim side, so I can always keep you believing I'm fabulous."

He laughed, the sound rumbling through her like distant thunder on a warm summer night.

"And because you're the best man I know," she

added, letting the truth shine in her eyes for the first time in as long as she could remember. "A man who, for some strange reason, really does believe in me."

He bent for another kiss. "Always, Charlie. Always."

* * * * *

*Look for more books in
Paula Graves's new miniseries,*
CAMPBELL COVE ACADEMY, *in 2017.*

*You'll find them wherever
Harlequin Intrigue books are sold!*

INTRIGUE

Available November 22, 2016

#1677 CARDWELL CHRISTMAS CRIME SCENE
Cardwell Cousins • by B.J. Daniels

Dee Anna Justice doesn't know what to make of private investigator Beau Tanner and the Cardwell family, who seem ready to welcome her with open arms. Her convict father says she needs to be protected from a deadly threat—but can she bring down her walls and let Beau in?

#1678 INVESTIGATING CHRISTMAS
Colby Agency: Family Secrets
by Debra Webb & Regan Black

Lucy Gaines walked away from sexy billionaire Rush Grayson before—the man who has it all seems to have no capacity for love. But when Lucy's sister and nephew are kidnapped, Rush is the only one who can save them and bring her family home for Christmas.

#1679 KANSAS CITY COUNTDOWN
The Precinct: Bachelors in Blue • by Julie Miller

Detective Keir Watson has seventy-two hours to identify the man terrorizing attorney Kenna Parker. Her amnesia makes identifying her stalker difficult. But trusting his growing feelings for the older woman? Impossible.

#1680 PHD PROTECTOR
The Men of Search Team Seven • by Cindi Myers

Nuclear scientist Mark Renfro has been kidnapped by a terrorist cell planning to detonate a nuclear bomb. On the verge of hopelessness, he meets Erin Daniels, the stepdaughter of his captor, whose life is also on the line. Only by working together can they escape, and the clock is ticking...

#1681 OVERWHELMING FORCE
Omega Sector: Critical Response • by Janie Crouch

Joe Matarazzo is the best hostage negotiator Omega Sector has ever seen. But when his ex-lover, lawyer Laura Birchwood, is in a stalker's sights, the situation may be more than even he can handle.

#1682 MOUNTAIN SHELTER
by Cassie Miles

When an international assassin targets neurosurgeon Jayne Shackleford, it's up to Dylan Simmons to keep her safe. A bodyguard and tech genius, Dylan understands Jayne's emotional isolation, and his safe house in the mountains just might have her letting down her defenses.

YOU CAN FIND MORE INFORMATION ON UPCOMING HARLEQUIN® TITLES, FREE EXCERPTS AND MORE AT WWW.HARLEQUIN.COM.

HICNM1116

INTRIGUE

DJ is about to gain a whole new family in order to escape the danger closing in from all sides in the latest addition to the Cardwell family saga.

Read on for a sneak preview of
CARDWELL CHRISTMAS CRIME SCENE,
the latest title from
New York Times *bestselling author B.J. Daniels.*

DJ Justice opened the door to her apartment and froze. Nothing looked out of place and yet she took a step back. Her gaze went to the lock. There were scratches around the keyhole. The lock set was one of the first things she'd replaced when she'd rented the apartment.

She eased her hand into the large leather hobo bag that she always carried. Her palm fit smoothly around the grip of the weapon, loaded and ready to fire, as she slowly pushed open the door.

The apartment was small and sparsely furnished. She never stayed anywhere long, so she collected nothing of value that couldn't fit into one suitcase. Spending years on the run as a child, she'd had to leave places in the middle of the night with only minutes to pack.

But that had changed over the past few years. She'd just begun to feel...safe. She liked her job, felt content here. She should have known it couldn't last.

The door creaked open at the touch of her finger, and she quickly scanned the living area. Moving deeper into the apartment, she stepped to the open bathroom door and glanced in. Nothing amiss. At a glance she could see the bathtub, sink and toilet as well as the mirror on the medicine cabinet. The shower door was clear glass. Nothing behind it.

That left just the bedroom. As she stepped soundlessly toward it, she wanted to be wrong. And yet she knew someone had been here. But why break in unless he or she planned to take something?

Or leave something?

Like the time she'd found the bloody hatchet on the fire escape right outside her window when she was eleven. That message had been for her father, the blood from a chicken, he'd told her. Or maybe it hadn't even been blood, he'd said. As if she hadn't seen his fear. As if they hadn't thrown everything they owned into suitcases and escaped in the middle of the night.

She moved to the open bedroom door. The room was small enough that there was sufficient room only for a bed and a simple nightstand with one shelf. The book she'd been reading the night before was on the nightstand, nothing else.

The double bed was made—just as she'd left it.

She started to turn away when she caught a glimmer of something out of the corner of her eye.

Don't miss CARDWELL CHRISTMAS CRIME SCENE by B.J. Daniels, available December 2016 wherever Harlequin® Intrigue books and ebooks are sold.

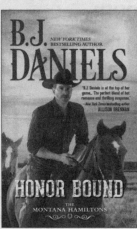

JUST CAN'T GET ENOUGH?

Join our social communities
and talk to us online.

You will have access to the latest
news on upcoming titles and special
promotions, but most importantly,
you can talk to other fans about your
favorite Harlequin reads.

Harlequin.com/Community

Facebook.com/HarlequinBooks

Twitter.com/HarlequinBooks

Pinterest.com/HarlequinBooks

THE WORLD IS BETTER WITH

Romance

Harlequin has everything from contemporary, passionate and heartwarming to suspenseful and inspirational stories.

Whatever your mood, we have romance when you need it, wherever you are!

HARLEQUIN®

A *Romance* FOR EVERY MOOD™

www.Harlequin.com

#RomanceWhenYouNeedIt

THE WORLD IS BETTER WITH

Romance

Harlequin has everything from contemporary, passionate and heartwarming to suspenseful and inspirational stories.

Whatever your mood,
we have a romance just for you!

Connect with us to find your next great read, special offers and more.

f /HarlequinBooks

@HarlequinBooks

www.HarlequinBlog.com

www.Harlequin.com/Newsletters

HARLEQUIN®

A *Romance* FOR EVERY MOOD™

www.Harlequin.com